Ultimate Rage – Ragnarok

Andrew Holten

Publisher: Andrew Holten
c/o Block Services
Stuttgarter Str. 106
D-70736 Fellbach
andrew.holten@gmx.net
www.andrewholtenmedia.com

Cover design: Buchcoverdesign.de / Chris Gilcher
https://buchcoverdesign.de

Image copyright: Adobe Stock ID 241951673, Adobe Stock ID 1698349, Adobe Stock ID 168585710, Adobe Stock ID 139446074, Adobe Stock ID 86505271, Adobe Stock ID 304576268 and freepik.com

1

They called it *nigger-beating*. Many of the victims were not even black, but some were. It didn't matter to them, because they were the ones who decided who was a nigger and who was not.

They had already chosen the next victims. For quite a while, they had been following the migrant couple, who were on their way home to the asylum seekers' home, taking the path through the forest.

Thomas shook his head. "There you see again how stupid these niggers are – and how arrogant. Didn't they learn in the bush that you don't just walk through the woods? Coming out here to us, thinking everything is fine. As if they own it all. They get a nice welcome. Get everything shoved up our asses that we have to work for. And of course, they believe that nothing can happen to them. Everything is always perfectly fine, because you couldn't be attacked by a dangerous animal at every corner here. Like hell you couldn't. We'll show them that there are predators here, too."

His buddies grinned. The fact that none of them really had to work had no place in their thoughts. Each of them had grown up in a financially independent family, had attended good schools, and truly didn't have to worry about the future. Nor were any of them in danger of losing their jobs.

But all that did not count, because their hatred was greater. A hatred that found more and more understanding in the country, because the climate had changed. What had been unthinkable years ago was now becoming an ever more widespread reality day by day, because xenophobic statements were increasingly considered socially acceptable, and not just since Trump was president. Yes, anyone who did not express criticism was even considered to belong to the system and to be in line with it. Didn't people see the great danger posed by all the strangers who were pouring into the country so easily? *Islamization*. The erosion of liberal values and democracy. The crimes committed by migrants, so that no one could dare walk the streets with peace of mind.

Thomas and his buddies wouldn't let that happen. They would do something and show the niggers that this was still their country. That they wouldn't stand for anything. They would protect their families. Their neighbors. Their people. And their homeland.

The two who took the shaded path through the forest as a matter of course were not the first and they would not be the last. They didn't like to pretend to be friendly and happy to be here, but Thomas and the others knew better. Each of them was dangerous, in one way or another. Potential rapists and carriers of diseases that had long since been eradicated in this advanced country. But also with the fact that they bring their rat spawn into the world here, for which of course the common taxpayer should pay. Or they mated with natives, in order to then produce half-breeds and thus contaminate more and more the pure blood of the people. And then there was their religion, which ordered them to kill all those of other faiths.

No, this had to be stopped before it was too late.

Apparently, the way directly through the forest had become a little too risky for the two, because they turned off and now walked along the road, which was better lit, but had no footpath.

Typical for such niggers, Thomas thought to himself and snorted. And if they then get knocked down, it was of course the driver's fault. Just because these degenerate savages had no idea where you were allowed to go as a pedestrian and where not. What traffic rules were. Oh, they probably even knew the rule, knew that you couldn't walk there, but they didn't care. The rules didn't apply to them. After all, they were guests in this country and behaved here as if they were in their bush. If they supposedly wanted to become citizens here, why didn't they follow the existing rules and laws? If they didn't do that in the country where they were and where one should show oneself from the best side just in their situation, how would that look later?

But if you pointed out to them that if you wanted to stay here, you had to abide by laws and not put yourself and certainly not others in danger, they can surely come up with some hypocritical explanations. About fear and so on. That the street was better lit. If they could speak the language here at all and not some Swahili or whatever the hell it was called. No one had forced them to be out so late at night. Why were they here at all? Shouldn't they instead be in their accommodation?

Thomas chewed on his lip and clenched his hands into fists. The more he watched the two, the angrier he became. They were truly a danger to the community. Everything had been fine until it had been decided to build this reception home. No one wanted it, but a number of the citizen representatives pretended that there would be broad support for it among the population. No one was asked. Probably some money had changed hands, which made this decision easier. And how quickly the thing had been thrown up. But still, homeless people had to sleep on the street. There was no such shelter built for them.

So much was going wrong. But Thomas and his friends would make sure that at least tonight something went right. Oh yes. They would teach those two a lesson that they would have been better off staying home. They would make an example that should be a lesson to the others. Especially to all those rapists for whom it was normal to molest and ravish women like in their home country.

Thomas grinned and pulled down his mask, which ensured that his victims always looked into a white, expressionless face. However, it was no longer as white as the first time. He had liked the way the blood smeared and clotted on the white plastic, so he didn't wipe it all off. On the forehead of the mask, between the eyeholes, he had drawn a swastika. It had been done in high spirits at a party after roughing up three unaccompanied youths. Of course, Thomas was not a Nazi. He had nothing to do with that stupid, right-wing rabble. He was just one of the concerned fellow citizens who no longer wanted to stand idly by while the government destroyed the entire country with its misguided policies. He would protect his family, friends and neighbors. In his town there were many old people who had worked hard all their lives and built this community, and who did not deserve to spend their twilight years in fear and terror.

Thomas took out his brass knuckles and slipped them over his right hand. He had specially padded the rings inside so that they didn't keep chafing his skin when he punched, which hurt like hell.

He also had his folding knife with him. The hunting folding knife with a high- quality-looking reddish-brown wooden handle and a blade length of almost four inches would serve its purpose when he cut the swastika into the bastard's cheek. On the forehead it did no good, as the nigger could grow hair that hung over it. But on the cheek, he couldn't hide that. He would have preferred to burn it into them, but that proved too complicated. That's where the knife was a good alternative, even if it wasn't a Bowie knife.

Again, the swastika was not proof that Thomas was a Nazi. It was useful because these foreign bastards knew just two things about it: here they got everything shoved up their asses and here there were Nazis. And they were something like the very worst specter for them. Unfortunately, it didn't stop them from staying away. But if it spread among them that this specter still existed and it cut its mark into one's flesh, then it certainly did not remain without effect. If it stopped just one more of these niggers from coming here, then it had already served its purpose.

Thomas saw Alex pull down his mask as well. His was one of a horror clown, which always had a great effect on these savages, perhaps even greater than Thomas's white, expressionless face. Ralph, for his part, wore his werewolf mask again, and Anton one with the face of Iron Man, since his real one, similar to Thomas's, had broken the last time.

"We're going to have to start catching these fuckers," Alex said, "or they'll be too close to the houses again in a minute."

Thomas nodded. Alex was right. There was no way he was going to let them get away. But they still had to be careful. If the two noticed them too early, they could escape faster on the paved road, since Thomas and the others were coming from the forest. Of course, this was not allowed to happen and would be devastating. Every one of them who escaped unpunished was another risk. But in a moment the opportunity would arise when the two had passed the next lantern and it became a little darker again between this one and the next. That was the ideal spot where there was no escape for the two. And then they would feel the retribution for having so easily invaded this peaceful community and making people feel unsafe in their homes.

Thomas smiled at the thought and reached once again for his left trouser pocket, where he had stowed his small grip pliers. He would use them again to get one tooth at a time. Maybe he would pull several, but he would take only one for his collection. He had once heard that in Vietnam, U.S. soldiers collected the ears of their slain enemies and wore them as necklaces. He had liked that. But such a thing would not be possible, of course, unfortunately. A tooth, however, seemed unproblematic to him and, moreover, a very nice souvenir.

Alex looked at Thomas. Both grinned under their masks, as the couple approached right in the middle between the two lanterns. The perfect point to finally strike.

Thomas could swear that they had timed it to within an inch of their lives when they crashed out of the undergrowth. The young woman could just about scream, but Thomas didn't care. The more important one was the young man, and he directly felt the blow of Alex's baseball bat.

When they had rushed out, the young man had placed himself directly in front of his girlfriend, thus depriving himself of the moment to build up a cover. Bunglers. Didn't they even teach them to fight where they came from? That's no way to protect someone who was important to you. Something like that really pissed Alex off.

As punishment, Alex's baseball bat hit him right in the stomach and the nigger jackknifed perfectly. Nevertheless, he still had the strength to lift his head, which directly brought him a blow from Thomas. For now, however, that was not enough for what they had set out to do. An example had to be made and that would certainly not be the case after just two blows. They had completely different plans.

The young woman had screamed once more when Thomas hit her boyfriend, but had then fallen silent as soon as Ralph grabbed her from behind and Anton stood up in front of her and snapped out his switchblade.

"You can play later," Thomas said. "First we have to get off the street."

With that, he and Alex grabbed the young man under the arms and dragged him into the forest. The young woman, however, resisted in desperation and repeatedly uttered a word that the four did not understand.

"Shut that bitch up already," said Thomas, "and drag her over here before we get discovered!"

Anton nodded, reared up in front of the woman and punched her in the face so hard that she not only stopped screaming, but slumped in Ralph's arms.

"There you go!" said Ralph and carried her backwards into the forest, while Anton took her feet to bring her to an area sparsely lit by a lantern. There they dropped her carelessly on the ground next to their friend. As if each other's presence revived them, they stirred.

"Well, well, well," Thomas said with a sneer, "they're still awake."

The young man said something to his girlfriend, who was crying softly. Only then did he turn to the four attackers, who with their masks looked like demons in the pale light. He raised his hand placatingly, which Alex was about to smash until every bone in it was broken several times. "Please," he pleaded. "No trouble!"

Thomas laughed. "You found him long ago!" With that, he pointed at Alex. "He's trouble. And I'm pain."

The young man looked at Thomas uncomprehendingly. "Don't understand."

Thomas shook his head. "That's exactly the problem. This arrogance and ignorance at that. Come to this country and don't understand anything. We're taught here that if you're going on vacation in another country, you should at least know some of the language there, out of courtesy. That goes without saying. But you want to live here. To participate in everything that our grandparents built, then our parents, and us too, while you have done none of that, except not bring your own country even close to that. That is why you are here. To take advantage of everything we've created. But do you at least speak the language of the country that will henceforth serve you with everything you want? No. You don't have to. On the contrary. We are supposed to learn your shitty language. Out of politeness. Out of respect. We're supposed to respect your culture, but you're not supposed to respect ours. You're here in our country, damn it. *You* have to adapt. Not us!"

The two migrants looked frightened into the emotionless face of the mask with the swastika on its forehead. They knew very little of the history of this country, but what this symbol meant, they knew. It was a terrible mark worn by the members of the evil in whose name they perpetrated inhuman atrocities in the past, but also now. And they were now defenselessly at their mercy.

"Don't understand," the young man repeated and tried to take his girlfriend, who was shaking all over, in his arms. Immediately Anton and Ralph were with them and pulled her away, while Thomas brought his masked face very close to his.

"Then we'll teach you some understanding!" he hissed. "Understanding that you shouldn't have come here, you fucking freeloaders!"

With that, he grabbed the young man by the collar and struck. His fist hit the man's face without stopping. The man's head swung back and blood spurted from his split lip.

Thomas let go of the dazed man, who simply slumped backwards. Thomas wiped at his mask. "Disgusting!" Then he looked down at his victim. "He's almost gone. All that nigger sportsmanship and shit. Here you see there's so nothin' to 'em."

"So what do we do now?" Alex wanted to know.

"Maybe we'll torch him a bit," Anton suggested. "Then he'll wake up all right."

"No, too dangerous," Thomas replied. "After that, the wanker will set the forest on fire. That won't do, since they're trying so hard to reforest it."

With that, he looked at the young woman. "But we still have the bitch. Let's get on with her first. The fucker will wake up again, then we'll take care of him."

Anton nodded and Ralph pulled the young woman to her feet and held her arms.

Thomas came closer and smiled under his mask. "For a black bitch, you actually have quite a pretty face. Might have white blood in you from when a colonist once mounted your great-great-great grandmother. You're spreading your legs for all to see, fucked up as you are. Flood the world with your rat spawn, like locusts. Without you there would be no famines and plenty of space on earth. Because of you and these fucking Islamists. These towelheads, who also multiply like rabbits, so that they can displace us. We know how it stands around the resources of the earth. But you guys just keep going unchecked and taking us down with you. You fucking niggers who want to destroy our culture!"

His mask was now close at hand, gazing into the young woman's terror-widened eyes as she shook her head again and again. Thomas grinned and feasted on her panic-filled sight. "You want to fuck? Then we'll fuck you. That's what you nigger bitches all want, isn't it?"

14

"Do you really want to fuck them?" asked Anton.

"Why not?" interjected Ralph. "She smells clean. And she's quite snug, isn't she?"

"But I don't want to get anything away from me. Who knows who's had his dick in her in the asylum center?"

Thomas turned to Anton. "I'm sure she's clean. Just look at her. They've given her all the care she needs, and I'm sure she's received full medical attention. Your grandma in the home can only dream of that. It's our right to fuck her. Like the colonists back then in Africa, who were allowed to take all the women as a thank you for trying to make something out of the filthy, backward continent. Unfortunately without success, as we know, because the savages were just too stupid and did not understand what they were doing good."

With that, he turned back to the young woman and grabbed her face. "But this cunt certainly complies with the good old purity law."

Anton didn't seem convinced. "But I want to see Sandra right away. She'll kill me if I get something from this bitch and give it to her."

"Then just use a rubber," Alex suggested.

Thomas nodded. "Exactly. And I bet her cunt is nice and tight. That will make you even hotter for Sandra and you'll really give it to her. Then Sandra will be happy too. You see, you all get something out of this."

Alex laughed. "Then you should hurry up. When me and my spanking are done with her, her cunt won't be very tight anymore. You'll have to fuck her in the ass. And whether it complies with the purity law, I doubt it. They don't know toilet paper where she's from." With that he stroked his baseball bat obscenely.

Thomas nodded, reached into his pocket and pulled out the folding knife, which he snapped open right in front of the young woman's face. Ralph threw her to her knees and she looked at everyone completely terrified, trembling all over.

"Strip!" Thomas ordered, twisting the knife back and forth.

The young woman did not move, only continued to look from one to the other with trembling lips.

"Strange," Thomas said. "Actually, you'd think she'd at least know the word after all, the little nigger bitch."

"Then I guess we'll have to be helpful to her after all and show her what we mean," Anton pressed out between angrily clenched teeth and grabbed her shirt to tug at it gruffly. The young woman screamed and tried to wriggle away, but this only made Anton angrier. In a sweeping motion, he struck her in the face with the back of his right hand. Her head was thrown to one side and she went down.

"Easy!" Alex interjected. "When she's unconscious, it's not so much fun. She's supposed to get something out of it and see everything nicely. Otherwise, the whole thing doesn't make any sense."

"That's right," Thomas confirmed. "After all, we want her to enjoy this to the fullest and learn something from it."

With that, Ralph tugged her back up and Thomas brought his mask very close to her face again. "Take it off."

He reached for her shirt and tugged lightly at it. Then at her skirt. "Take it off."

"I think she needs a little encouragement," Alex said, and then kicked her still unconscious friend in the side.

The young woman screamed and she wanted to rush to her friend's aid, but Ralph held her back.

"Undress!" Thomas repeated. "Well, you should really understand what we want from you. It can't be that difficult, even for someone like you!"

Alex laughed and kept slapping the baseball bat into his free palm.

The young woman looked alternately at Thomas, Alex and Anton, gazed with trembling lips into their demonic-looking grimaces and finally reached for her shirt.

Thomas nodded. "There you go. There you go. You understand us just fine. Certainly such words as undressing, cocksucking, and fucking, anyway."

He was just stepping a little closer to the young woman again when something rammed into Alex. It happened so fast that everyone just jumped to the side, but Ralph didn't let go of the young woman.

When Thomas turned around, he saw only a shadowy figure sitting on Alex and beating him furiously. At first Thomas thought her friend had woken up again, but he was still lying unconscious in the same place as before.

Anton was the first to react and jumped towards the figure. The figure, however, had apparently been waiting for him, snatched his baseball bat from Alex and smashed it with full force against Anton's right knee. A brutal crunch gave the impression of splintered bones and Anton cried out in pain. But even as he went down, the figure stood up, swinging the baseball bat around so that Anton's head was hit by it as it fell. There was something deeply repulsive about the crunch.

Thomas thought he saw Anton's shattered lower jaw detach itself from his head, but it was only his imagination. Anton plopped down like a wet sack on the floor, where he lay twitching.

"Fuck!" Ralph groaned, still holding the young woman, who looked transfixed at what was happening, seemingly unable to believe that two of her attackers had been struck down.

"Who the hell are you?" Thomas groaned, but the figure did not move. Because of the dim light he could not make out its features. But the figure was tall and appeared to be a man, dressed in dark colors and his face obscured by a hood pulled low.

Thomas jumped forward, ready to hit the attacker first with his killing stick and then let him feel the blade. However, the still motionless figure slid to the side at the last moment and Thomas felt a fist rammed right into his face. His nose broke like a toothpick and blood shot out, hitting the mask and splashing up into his eyes, taking away the last of his vision. In the next moment the baseball bat crashed into his stomach and Thomas was thrown back by the force. Only peripherally did he notice how the knife slipped from his hand and he crashed to the ground.

"Shit!" yelled Ralph, pushing the young woman in the direction of the unknown assailant and running. The stranger threw the baseball bat at him, hitting him in the back. He stumbled and crashed into a tree. He groaned and turned, ready to strike. But even as he turned, the stranger's fist was waiting for him, sending the back of his head crashing into the tree.

Immediately Ralph wanted to stand up again, when with full force the knee of the stranger crashed into his testicles, which felt as if they had been burst open. As his body reflexively folded forward, the same knee hit him in the head, causing it to crash against the tree again.

Dazed, Ralph saw how the stranger tore off his mask and in the next moment his fist crashed into his face again. And again. And again. And again, shattering his nose bone, his cheekbones, his jaw. Then the flat palms of his hands crashed simultaneously on his ears. When his eardrums burst, Ralph just blacked out.

Thomas turned onto his back and breathed heavily. He tore off his mask to wipe his eyes clean. In doing so, he came to his broken nose, which hurt like hell. So did his ribs, some of which were surely broken.

The stranger approached him, picking up the baseball bat as he did so.

Thomas raised his hands defensively. "Hey!" he groaned, already suspecting what was about to happen.

Like an unstoppable force of nature, the stranger made a lunge, swinging the baseball bat, which crashed with unrestrained force against Thomas's left hand, shattering every single bone. The fingertips of Thomas's right hand were also hit, causing the fingers to bend backwards and break.

Thomas screamed out. The attacker swung the baseball bat hard on Thomas's knee. Again and again. Then swung the bat with all his might on Thomas's testicles.

Lying down, Thomas threw up and barely managed to turn to his side so that he could get some of the vomit out of his mouth. His body was a single wound, shattered and in total pain. He was shaking all over and felt himself losing control of his bowels.

When he looked up again, the stranger was standing over him. In one hand he held Thomas's mask, which he seemed to be looking at, in the other his jackknife.

"Who are you?", Thomas still brought forth in a quivering voice drenched in utter despair.

The stranger dropped the mask and squatted on Thomas's torso, almost making the his eyes bulge out.

"I... am you!" the stranger said in an ominous voice.

For a brief moment, Thomas caught a glimpse of the stranger's face and it startled him more than anything he had ever seen.

Then the stranger grabbed Thomas's hair with his left hand and pulled his head up. With a horrified look, Thomas saw the stranger bring the knife to his forehead. As the blade cut into his flesh, Thomas cried out. He knew exactly what symbol the stranger would use to mark him forever.

2

Mo first had to lean forward when he entered the apartment. He was only in his early thirties and yet he already felt so old. Soon he would no longer be able to use his nickname Mo, which truly belonged to a young, dynamic man. His real name, Mohamed, was probably more appropriate, since everyone would then automatically see an old man sporting a full gray beard. He didn't have the full beard yet, but he was thinking about growing one, but of course much shorter and more modern.

He was simply taking on too much, which is why he was panting now. But the stress in his job was enormous and somewhere he needed an outlet. But it wasn't just work. Sometimes there were days when frustration about everything boiled over and demanded a reaction. Only lately it wasn't just days, but more like weeks.

He straightened up and took a breath. He really needed to shower and make himself presentable again. His customers expected a certain appearance and right now he didn't look very confidence-inspiring. More like the incarnation of one of the nightmares they had, and he couldn't afford that.

He always had to be doubly careful that people at least forgot with their second thoughts that he was of Turkish descent and thus shed all their prejudices and dislikes, at least for a second, so that he could win them over, step by step. That their first thought was simply "Turk" and thus an imprinted continuous fire of prejudice hammered itself into their brain, he knew.

Therefore, he built on the second thought to gradually work his way forward.

Mo took another breath, then smiled. Someone during his training had once explained to him what a positive effect it had if you simply smiled for a minute. It was better to do that when you were alone, because people around you would think it odd if you just smiled, but Mo could confirm for himself that it helped.

Turks were said to often look so grim, as if they were constantly looking for a sign of provocation. You couldn't say that about Mo. His facial expression was always friendly, relaxed and inviting. This had mostly to do with that smile exercise that had already become routine for him. But few people knew what kind of volcano was bubbling inside him.

Yesterday he had overdone it and paid the receipt today. His fists still hurt and showed abrasions on some knuckles. Not good. As a customer service representative in a bank, you had to make sure you looked neat. Whether the body was fully covered with tattoos under the suit didn't matter, as long as they didn't see it. But anything that was uncovered had to conform to certain rules, guidelines and expectations. And if someone asked, he would simply say he had fallen off his bike. That sounded plausible and always went over well. People in small towns in the countryside liked it when you were environmentally conscious and didn't take the car. It was clear to everyone that accidents like this happened.

Mo looked at his smiling face in the mirror. Yes, it really looked crazy. As if he was trying to be the Turkish version of the Joker. That was all that was missing, that he was associated not only with all the negative characteristics of a Turk, but also with a homicidal psychopath. Otherwise, he looked quite friendly and, moreover, good-looking. In order not to reveal that he had a well-trained body, he would have had to wear a potato sack. His face truly had something very mischievously friendly about it, which won him sympathy from women of all ages. With his three-day beard, thick curly black hair, dark eyes and good teeth, he looked very attractive. Almost like a model.

Mo startled when he heard a noise. Unmistakably, someone was in his apartment. Immediately his whole body tensed up and switched into fight mode. Once trained, you couldn't get rid of such fighter instincts. You could suppress them, overplay them, but they were always there.

All his senses were now on alert, searching for any indication of where the enemy was lurking and from where he would strike. Cautious as a tiger moving slowly toward its prey, Mo crept silently forward. As he did so, he kept his left arm bent, his hand loose to allow him to react flexibly, while his right hand was drawn back and clenched into a fist, ready to spring forward in a veritable explosion of power. Whoever had dared to break in on him would be in for a nasty surprise.

Mo wished he had immediately parted with his sweater and T-shirt underneath, both of which were drenched in sweat and could become a disadvantage in a fight. Besides, it would have had something of Bruce Lee style if he had crept along with a naked, muscle-bound upper body to face his opponent.

Mo's opponent appeared abruptly and just as silently as Mo himself. Mo, however, was prepared, his opponent was not. With a battle cry that went to the marrow of his bones, the like of which even an Asian karate fighter could not produce more intensely, Mo lunged at the figure, swept its legs away, and a moment later pinned it to the ground, pressing its own hands behind its back.

"Ow!" was all the figure uttered.

"Give up!" Mo countered when he noticed the man below him trying to free his hands.

"Why?" came the somewhat surprising answer.

"Because you have no arms to fight with. And your legs are also useless."

"I'll blind you with spit!" the man replied, sounding undaunted.

Nothing happened for a few moments, during which the figure breathed a little heavily under Mo's weight. Then they both laughed and Mo stood up, helping the man up and hugging him joyfully.

"Ben! I wasn't expecting you today!" Mo greeted his longtime friend and looked at him with a smile. Ben hadn't changed and still looked as unassuming and almost gangly as ever, which of course was completely deceiving. It was even more possible to fall for this mistake if Ben hadn't been grooming his short but thick full beard for years, without which he reminded everyone directly of John Cusack.

Ben smiled. "I was able to get away early and thought I'd surprise you."

Mo slapped Ben lightly on the shoulder. "You succeeded."

Ben nodded and looked at Mo. "Well, maybe I should have waited until after the shower to do that. Are you working out that hard again?" With that, he pointed to the large punching bag that stood in the corner of Mo's living room and had clearly lost its color in some places.

Mo shrugged his shoulders.

"Not going so well right now, I guess," Ben stated. There was no accusation in his words, but rather a very accurate knowledge, so Mo didn't even try to fool Ben. Again he shrugged his shoulders.

"The work. And all the other crap. You know."

Ben nodded, then looked at Mo's damaged knuckles. "Any incidents?" They both smiled mirthlessly and Mo waved it off.

"Nothing serious. You know I keep my head down and out of trouble. Just find it hard sometimes. Not like when I was younger. But sometimes, well, I have to blow off steam. But if I wasn't careful, I'm sure you would have heard something."

Ben smiled and this time it was genuine and much friendlier. "It's okay. I just don't want you to get in danger or break what you've built. You can be really proud of that."

Mo nodded with a smile. "We both can. What about you?"

Now it was Ben's turn to look noncommittal. "Oh, you know. I've finally settled down."

Mo continued to look at Ben. "And you expect me to believe that? No harm done? No more nightmares?"

Ben smiled wryly. "They'll never go away, I guess. But I have to live with that. And I can, thanks to you and your family."

Mo laughed. "I guess we both saved ourselves, brother." In Turkish, it was often customary for good friends to call each other brother. Mo never did, but he meant it the same way with Ben. Ben was more than a friend to him, he was his brother.

"So, are you going to join us?" Mo finally wanted to know. With that, he as- ked the big question that was always in the room.

Ben went to the kitchen and prepared the coffee. "Where I am, I feel comfortable. The big one, you know, doesn't suit me so well."

Ben laughed. "Well, we're not that big. Just closer to the center of power. Today at the meeting you can take a look at everything. Whereas, hmm, if you see the bosses, maybe you'll stay right where you are."

"Which would be perfectly fine."

Mo raised his hands placatingly. "Of course. Of course. But isn't your clientele slowly dying off? And I think the small outlying branches are bound to be the first to close."

Ben turned on the coffee maker and didn't look over at Mo. "I'll see. I'm already doing customer visits. Like to drive around, too."

"Yes, the lone knight on his heroic quest to make the world a little better. Still the same old."

Ben smiled. "Not quite the old man."

Mo came over to Ben and put his right hand on his shoulder. "You've always been like this. Don't forget that. There is no before and after. The after was only because you were like this before. You have nothing to blame yourself for. You wrestle with your demons as I wrestle with mine. There is nothing wrong with that. We just must never give up the fight and let them win."

"No retreating. No giving up."

"That's right, brother. That's right. Blood of my blood. Always."

Ben laughed and raised his right arm to expose a spot just below his wrist that showed a fine white line. "We were already two goofballs. If you did something like that today, you'd be declared completely insane. *Hey, become my blood brother. Sure, and how? Easy, we take the totally germy knife here, cut ourselves on our forearms, and then hold the wounds together.*"

Mo laughed. "Did you catch an infection or did I? So much for pure blood. Mine was pure, because nothing happened to you when you got it. But your sauce was probably totally contaminated with bacteria, and I, poor Turk, got something from you right away."

Ben laughed. "You really can't tell anyone!" Then he took a breath and looked at Mo for a few silent moments. "I wonder what your father saw in me. I mean, I..."

Mo smiled graciously. "He saw in you exactly the same as I do."

Ben grinned. "Not exactly."

"Yeah well, at first I thought my dad was crazy and just wanted to beat the shit out of you. Okay, I was young and didn't know any better. Turkish blood and puberty is a dangerous mixture. You need a little more time. But if it wasn't for you, I'd be in jail or worse right now. I owe you my life, man. And I'm sorry I was so angry at the beginning. At you and at my father. I was a stupid Turk. That's how we are sometimes."

Ben laughed. "It has nothing to do with being a Turk. You find that far too often and unfortunately everywhere."

Mo playfully bumped Ben's chest and instantly went into the stereotypical cocky macho pose, speaking with an exaggerated accent. "What are you saying? Is it supposed to be because of me? Want stress or what?"

They both laughed, but Ben quickly became serious again. "No, honestly. I keep thinking about why he did that."

Again, Mo held his friend by the shoulder. "Hey, man. You need to put this behind you already. You don't owe my father or me anything. My father, our father, was a damn good man. Better than either of us dumbasses will ever be. And he always saw the good in people, even in the worst places. The fact that we both became something decent and are still working on ourselves would make him proud."

Ben nodded and then pulled an exaggeratedly thoughtful face. "Well, I'm sure he'd be proud of me. But of you? Well."

Mo playfully nudged Ben's chest. "Let's have breakfast. You totally slowed me down. No respect for a hardworking man who needs his food."

"We're going to my branch first before we then move on to the convention," Mo explained. "It may not look like much, but it's where the big deals are made. Customers prefer the ambience as opposed to the large and very impersonal-looking big buildings. Actually, you'd think that our boss in particular wouldn't care, but he personally lobbied to keep the store. Such a small, insignificant branch. Why?"

Ben frowned and looked at Mo, who was sitting behind the wheel of his naturally immaculate-looking Mercedes. "Have you found an explanation for this by now? Did you perhaps hide the Amber Room in a safe in the basement?"

Mo's put-on laugh showed Ben that his best friend wasn't entirely dismissing the idea.

"I really have no idea. It's definitely weird. And that's why I've been doing research."

Mo was silent for a moment. "I don't know," he continued, shaking his head. "Must be Dad's bad influence. Must have given me that much-vaunted cop gene, though he was always glad I didn't follow in his footsteps. Or you."

He was silent again for a moment. "It's such a tingle. Ever since I overheard Ahrend lobbying to keep the store open, I've always looked at it with different eyes. Because... why is he doing this? It's as if there's something hidden in it somewhere that I can't grasp. As if there's an invisible veil that neither I nor anyone else can penetrate, and we only see appearances."

Ben nodded. "Then you're guessing that your branch, of all places, is some- thing like the Vatican Bank."

"Ha-ha, very funny. No, I don't know what it is. But I think it's unlikely that Ahrend has the welfare of small investors in mind. He became a banker because he loves money. And he's a total career guy because that's how he gets even more money."

Ben nodded. "Sounds sympathetic."

"Yes. One of those belongs in the big corporate offices. And yet he shows up at our place almost regularly. He's almost sharing an office with my colleague Anna."

Ben grinned. "Ah, *the* Anna."

"Yeah, stop it. You know there's nothing going on. But you'd think there was something going on between the two of them. With him, I wouldn't be surprised.

He's really after anything in a skirt. But with her I can't imagine that. And when you see the two of them... nah. You can see right away that the guy is not sympathetic to Anna. I mean, I know a few things about her that just speak against it. I'm not sure, though."

Ben shrugged his shoulders. "Maybe it's as simple as that. The guy has a thing for this Anna and wants to keep the opportunity to visit her as unobserved as possible. Wouldn't be the first guy to take advantage of his position of power. And from the way you describe her, she does seem like a very respectable woman."

Mo smiled wryly. "She really is. Under other circumstances, I'd do anything to end up with her. But we're really just colleagues."

"So you think there's another box going on. Mob money. Embezzlement. Trump's secret assets."

Mo laughed and shook his head. "Oh, man. If anyone catches on that I told you about this, I can get myself a rope right now. Then there goes my career."

Ben smiled slightly. "Don't worry. I know how to keep a secret."

Mo's expression became much friendlier again. "I know that, brother. I know that all too well. I don't know. Maybe I'll show you what I've got sometime. I haven't shown anyone yet, because I don't really know what kind of spirit I'm chasing. I don't care. I'm still missing something. I'll get it and then I'll show you everything."

"All right, Mister Bond." Mo laughed out.

"More like Ethan Hunt from *Mission: Impossible*."

Ben got out and first looked around with a smile. "Nothing has really changed much here."

Mo nodded and looked around as well. "The sign is new. Was just put up two years ago."

Ben nodded. "Then you can't close the branch either, otherwise it wouldn't have been worth the investment in the first place."

With that, he looked around again. He had been here years ago the last time and had seen directly that he could certainly have felt at home here. But this was Mo's home, his workplace. He and Mo were close, very close in fact, had truly grown up like brothers since their early youth. Mo was his family, the only one he still had. But by the same token, Ben knew the urge inside himself to want to be alone. As much as he liked having Mo and meeting up with him, he was also happy to be alone most of the time.

The branch stood in the outskirts of the city, in a place that was rather village-like, even if there weren't as many farms here as there once were. The streets were clean, as were the houses, but everything was just as obviously old. There were smaller stores here and there, even still a travel agency, and Ben wondered how it managed to keep going here. The bank branch itself consisted of the ground and basement floors of a three-story building. The other floors were occupied by apartments and a doctor's office.

Ben noticed how his subconscious automatically scanned the surroundings. Instinctively, his eyes involuntarily searched the roofs, windows and entrances, analyzing all the information in the blink of an eye and classifying people according to their potential danger. He took a breath and closed his eyes. Then he smiled. Old habits that had become part of one's body and blood were hard to shake off. For that reason alone, he should stay away from Mo. The latter certainly understood, but he shouldn't be constantly confronted with Ben's spleens, as he called them. It was bad enough that he had to.

Even though the facade made it seem otherwise, the interior of the store was up to date and looked like everything had been renovated just recently. The color scheme was bright with sunny colors. Everything looked inviting and might have been a better fit for the travel agency across the street. The fact that difficult financial decisions were often made here and that incredible sums of money were handled, especially in the glassed-in individual offices, was not apparent from the rooms. This was not surprising, because since the financial crisis, people have been very suspicious of banks, suspecting them to be the lair of rapacious evil.

There wasn't really anything going on in the store. The employees present were sitting behind the counter at their respective desks, going about their work. When Ben and Mo entered the large room, they just looked up, smiled and raised their hands in greeting.

Whether anyone was working in the individual glazed offices could only be guessed at, since the panes were opaque up to a height of about 6 feet and thus not really transparent. Nevertheless, one seemed to have a good view into the main room, because the door to one office opened and a young woman stepped out, who was insignificantly younger.

Ben had to look twice. The very attractive slim woman with the dream measurements of 36-24-36, complete with blood-red hair tied in a simple braid, came up to them smiling. She wore a dark blue skirt that was knee-length, a white blouse and a jacket that matched the skirt. Her high heels topped it off and made her legs seem infinite despite her height of about 5 foot 3.

"Oh," Ben just let out softly.

"Yep," Mo confirmed and smiled.

When Mo's colleague stood in front of them, she extended her hand to Ben,
who accepted it.

"May I introduce my esteemed colleague and also the boss here, Anna Kerkov," Mo explained. "And this young man is Ben Becker. One of our many hard-working employees doing service for the little guy on the prairies around the country."

Anna nodded. "Ben Becker. Yes, I've heard a lot about you. Mo here really wants you to join us. He's been communicating that since he started here. I thought at first he was going to use the flower to sort of declare he was gay and get his partner here."

Ben grinned and this intensified when he saw Mo's horrified face.

"Gay? Me? You can't seriously say something like that to a Turk."

Anna remained unimpressed and did not avert her gaze from Ben. "Mo, you were born here and know Turkey mainly from your two-week childhood vacations. Even your father was a kid when he came here and barely spoke Turkish all his life, as you always point out."

Mo folded his arms. "There you see it, brother, why Turkish men only flirt with women, give them orders or boss them around. Because when a Turk really talks to a woman, tells her about himself, family and stuff, it just leads to trouble. Because a woman will always use it against you. Always."

Ben laughed and Anna joined in. "Yes, emancipation is already hard to digest for a macho Turkish man. And you're something like his half-brother?"

"No, my real brother," Mo improved.

"Yes," Anna confirmed. "I never really understood your connection that way."

Ben smiled vaguely. "Mo's family was kind enough to take me in when I was a teenager. They always made me feel that I was one of them."

Anna nodded in understanding. "Difficult childhood."

It was more of a statement than a question and Ben nodded.

"You could say that."

"Mo doesn't talk much about it, more like nothing."

"Which I'm also very grateful for."

Anna smiled in understanding and then clapped her hands. "But now you're

here in our little outpost. You've been here before?"

Ben nodded. "Yes, when Mo started here. But they weren't here then. Besides, I remember the store from before."

Anna laughed. "Yes, I have been here. But I have a lot of outside appointments. Honestly, it's not really mine. I prefer to be in my office and rule the world from there. So I'm glad that Mo takes these appointments off my hands – he seems to mind such things far less. And they say it's one of your favorite things to do. We could really use someone like that. And right now, the chances of promotion are not bad."

Mo smiled and put an arm around Ben's shoulders. "Unfortunately, our Ben here is just the opposite of a career guy and perfectly content where he is. I guess I'll have to work him a little more to make something of it."

Anna nodded. "Do that. I'd definitely be open to it, because if this is all maintained, which I assume it will be, we can use people like you."

"Who can we use?" a loud voice suddenly rang out.

Before Ben turned around, he saw Anna's facial expression change. All at once, her entire friendly aura had disappeared and a flash appeared in her eyes that Ben didn't know how to interpret.

Then he saw the man who had entered the store who looked as if he owned the place. The man, about mid-fifties, was as tall as Ben and Mo, but he looked like he was twice as heavy. His tailored gray suit was taut, but the good cut concealed everything. The moustache was conspicuous, as was the half-bald head, shining with sweat, as if he had walked all the way here, which Ben doubted.

Mo didn't have to say anything, because Ben knew who it was: Guenther Ahrend, the immediate boss of Mo and Anna.

"Hello, everyone. I thought I would stop by before the big meeting. After all, I know how precarious the parking situation is with us, so I wanted to offer you, Ms. Kerkov, a ride with me. I have a company parking lot there and we could take the opportunity to talk about some things I wanted to clarify with you."

Everyone acted as if such a thing was perfectly normal, smiled and nodded. Ben could feel Anna's tension, and noticed that her smile did not transfer to her eyes.

"With pleasure, Mr. Ahrend. I'll just get my bag. By the way, may I introduce you to Mr. Ben Becker. He works in one of our field offices and we're hoping to get him to join us here."

Mr. Ahrend smiled as if he saw in Ben a famous South American soccer star he could sign, not a lowly employee he could direct to change jobs here with just one conversation with Ben's supervisor.

"Very nice, young man. We can always use capable people here. I'm sure you'll be at the meeting, too, so you'll hear all about what we're planning around here. I hope you will like it, I certainly will. Mrs. Kerkov, can we go then?"

Anna gave another forced smile and then went into her office. Ahrend looked after her unabashedly, his gaze being directed primarily at her buttocks and legs. When Anna came back and now had a much better grip on her mirthless smile, he also didn't miss the opportunity to put his hand on her back, placing it too low for Ben's liking.

When Ahrend's swanky Mercedes was gone, Ben looked into Mo's enraged face.

"Do you know what I mean now?"

Ben just nodded.

Mo took that nod. "Something is going on. Something very strange. And I have a very, very bad feeling about it. But I need proof first. And I'll get it."

"If there are any..." Ben indicated.

Mo nodded and looked inside the store. "Don't worry. If there are, I'll find them."

When they sat together in the evening to watch a movie together, Ben quickly noticed that his friend wasn't paying attention. Mo was staring at the tv screen, not taking in what was happening, and didn't seem to be there at all.

"We don't have to look at anything," Ben finally said.

"What?" Mo replied, as if he had just woken up from a trance and needed to get his bearings. He looked at Ben as if he had to figure out who he was first. Finally, he smiled apologetically and rubbed his hands over his face. "I'm really sorry, bro. I guess I'm just not really with it. This whole thing is really getting under my skin. I've known Anna for a while and worked with her a lot, including overtime. That's when you get to chatting, and that's when she told me a lot of things. She may not seem like it, but she's really been through a lot of shit. With all that dirt, she's truly to be admired for being where she is now. And then some asshole like Ahrend comes along and shamelessly takes advantage of his position. But why she goes along with it is beyond me. Ever since he started showing up regularly, she's been totally closed off to me, too."

Ben nodded. "And you're afraid Ahrend has something on her? Or involved in something?"

Mo took a breath. "In fact, I'm afraid it's worse than that. That he's been taking advantage of her for a long time. Abusing her." He shook his head. "I have to stop this." With that, he stood up.

"Where are you going?" asked Ben, surprised.

"Don't be mad at me, but I just have to go around the block again. I've been doing that a lot lately.

Jogging. To work out. Through the woods. Clear my head."

Ben laughed. "Through the woods – alone?"

Mo laughed as well. "Hey, I'm a big Turk and I can take care of myself."

Ben nodded. "Promise me you won't go looking for trouble. Just to release your frustration."

Mo acted overly innocent. *"Moi?* I wouldn't do something like that. Sounds totally out of character for me. But what am I supposed to do when trouble comes looking for me? You know yourself that some truly go for it, and then it's hard to ignore."

Ben took a breath. "Yes. Even in a village like this."

"Well, when I see something like that, I don't stay still. Have you heard about the four Nazi assholes? They've been ambushing, beating up and severely abusing, even raping, poor immigrants and people whose skin color was different, over and over again for months. Well, this went on until recently, when they met someone who really roughed them up. They'll probably never be able to ambush anyone again. They got really badly ripped apart. And in the end, each of them had a swastika cut into their forehead."

Ben remained silent and held Mo's gaze. Mo looked deeply into his eyes. "Have you heard about this?"

Ben nodded. "It's been all over the papers and the tv, after all."

"Yes, there was no getting around the news. Especially because there were similar incidents elsewhere. A local politician who belongs to the extreme right- wing scene was attacked in his home. He had made some really nasty statements and held some particularly perfidious views. Now he will have trouble getting out a sentence at all without spit running out of his mouth all the time. His jaw is all smashed up from someone hitting him with a hammer. Not to mention his right arm, which he will never be able to raise again for the leader salute, let alone use for anything else. Happened not too far from here. So I guess I'm not one of the ones to worry about, am I?"

Ben remained serious at first, then smiled. "Who knows? Ultraconservative Muslims aren't exactly known for their affability and unconditional charity, after all."

Mo smiled mirthlessly. "Unfortunately true. There are those, too. But the one who did it seems to be very specialized. He can't stand right-wing trash."

"Who can?"

"Too many, unfortunately," Mo agreed. "Too many. I blame it all on Trump." Then his smile became friendlier again. "Anyway, I'm going to take a quick shower and then I'll be gone for a while. Don't worry about me."

Ben raised his right eyebrow questioningly. "You're going to shower first?"

Mo nodded. "Yeah, call it spleen. It makes me feel better. Got it from an ex, she used to do it all the time. Well, sort of."

"About?"

Mo fussed. "Yes. Because before the shower came sex."

Ben laughed. "Don't look at me like that! I'm not going to help you there!"

Mo posed exaggeratedly and gave his voice a completely exaggerated, stereotypical accent. "Are you saying I'm gay or what? Watch it. I'll fuck you hard, dude!" Then he laughed and disappeared into the bathroom.

When he returned after the refreshing shower in full workout gear including hoodie, Ben was sitting on the sofa engrossed in a book. Mo smiled. "Still *Fool on the Hill*?"

Ben smiled. "Always have it with me." The book deals with the ancient battle of good versus evil.

"Have you identified with the Ragnarok character by now?"

Ben nodded. "I've had that from the beginning, ever since you told me about it and I read it."

"Great. Then I'll call you Ragnarok from now on."

Ben screwed up his face. "I'd rather you didn't."

"Why? I do it all the time anyway. Because ever since I first read the book, I always thought of you as Ragnarok, whatever name you chose."

Ben remained silent.

Mo smiled good-naturedly. "Don't worry about it, brother." He patted Ben on the shoulder. "I'm off now. You get a nice sleep." With that he disappeared out the door.

Ben looked at the closed door and then back at the open book. *Ragnarok*.

3

Sergey was sitting in his car, from which he had a view of both the front entrance and the back entrance of the bank. Fortunately for him, both entrances were each well lit by a streetlight, while no one would notice him sitting in the car.

It was the third night he'd spent like this, but the Administrator had given him clear instructions, believing that this Mohamed Aslan could show up here.

Sergey did not take orders from many people. For many years, the only exception had been his mother. Teachers and educators had never had anything worthwhile to say to him, unless his mother had told him to listen to her.

This was not because his mother had been particularly violent and had inflicted cruel punishments on him if he did not do what she said. He had heard of completely different experiences related by the other children, stories no one would ever believe. No, he listened to his mother because she was the only one he believed really loved him. Basically, she had always been a very fragile person, often sick because the heating kept breaking down. Nevertheless, she never complained, and also never said a bad word about her son.

His father had been different. He was a brutal man who ruled with iron force and on one occasion even beat his still young son to unconsciousness. But as Sergey later learned, what didn't kill you really made you tougher. And so one day he struck back.

He might not agree with his father in anything, with the exception of the penchant for raw, brutal violence along with an unbridled strength he had inherited. Without batting an eye, he broke almost every bone in his father's body. Only his father's incredible strength allowed him to survive.

But at the veterans' home, where he was slowly recovering from his injuries, no one expected that someone might have a reason to break in. So, the security conditions were understandably lax and it was easy for Sergey to break in. Again he broke every already healed bone of his father and then escaped again. He repeated this several times until the next time his father was waiting for him with a gun. He managed to put three shots into his son's body, but that did not stop Sergey from snatching the pistol from him and using it to beat his father up so brutally that for the rest of his life he was just a drooling creature that could no longer move, and even worse, articulate. Sergey hoped his father's mind had survived the attack, unable to draw attention to itself in any way and thus doomed to be trapped in his body.

After this final attack, Sergey allowed himself to be arrested without resistance and would have endured his execution without protest. But the state had other plans for him. They saw potential in him that should not be wasted. If one was capable of such unscrupulous deeds even at a young age, untrained, what would it look like when Sergey trained? And so the then still teenager was declared dead and put into a special commando unit, in which Sergey's innate abilities were perfected and used for their own purposes.

Sergey was never the scalpel you took out when you wanted to work particularly finely. He was the sledgehammer that was supposed to send unmistakable messages. He always proceeded with extreme brutality and unstoppably, which earned him the nickname "Terminator". However, no one had Arnold Schwarzenegger in mind, but rather Robert Patrick's T-1000, which also corresponded more to Sergey's stature and appearance – he had less oversized muscles, but rather an athletic figure.

For many years Sergey had served the Russian secret organization that carried out killing missions all over the world. He was always the one involved when it was supposed to look like a hit-and-run accident, a robbery, or burglary resulting in death. This was his specialty. Although he had truly been trained in all types of killing, people were very keen to avail of his rough, brutal style, which truly made every death look as if the victim had fallen to an overzealous petty criminal and not a professional killer.

Anyone who was that good would eventually attract the attention of the private sector. Since money was always a very good argument for persuasion, the conditions were quickly clarified. From time to time, he still worked for the military, which he did on the one hand out of patriotism and on the other hand because he owed them a lot. Nevertheless, he was of course paid very well for his services.

However, he carried out this order without being paid, since it was also convenient for him that the secrets did not become public.

When Sergey saw Mo's Mercedes, he had to smile. The Administrator had been right. Sergey liked people who were professionals, who could think strategically and put themselves in the shoes of others. The Administrator was able to do this, so he hadn't just let Sergey guard the branch on a whim, and he was right.

Nodding in acknowledgement, Sergey took out his smartphone and called the number he knew, which he used very rarely but knew by heart.

"He's here," he shared only briefly.

The Administrator hesitated before answering in a distorted voice that always reminded Sergey of Batman. He liked the idea of Batman himself giving him orders to kill, even if this was to be the first time. "Regrettable. Do what you have to do. But not in the bank. That draws too much attention to it. Get me whatever he's carrying."

Sergey did not need any more instructions. He understood. Even though he had never met the Administrator personally, he trusted him blindly. And the Administrator also knew Sergey and his qualities and thus held back with further explanations.

Why the Administrator basically gave him a kill order for the first time, he didn't care. This Mohamed Aslan, called Mo, posed a threat to their business relationship and had to be liquidated. Basically, the job was no different from his usual ones and would perhaps even be a lot easier.

Sergey got out of his car and continued to hide in the shadows. He would have liked to smoke a cigarette, but that would have been too conspicuous. He let his eyes wander over the houses, looking for suspicious movements. He wasn't really expecting it, but he had been trained to always expect the unexpected and never to feel too safe.

As Mo opened the back door to the store, he took another look around. There was no one to be seen anywhere. In a village like this, it was no wonder, since the proverbial sidewalks were deserted very early here and everything lay there as if abandoned. Now and then, one could see a few young people who came in the evening or at night along the streets, mostly coming from a party. However, this was not the case today.

When he entered the branch, he refrained from turning on the light. This was not because he was virtually breaking in here, but rather because neighbors could see the light if they happened to look outside and, in their righteousness, would call the police because someone might be stealing their money from their bank.

Since Mo knew the branch like the back of his hand, he had no trouble getting to Anna's office without a light. If someone asked him why he had been at the bank at that time, he would simply claim insomnia. He had often remarked on this and it was also known from previous places of work that he often worked at night. When you belonged to a team that also did business worldwide, this was not surprising.

Mo was sweating. He knew he was doing the right thing, but even the right thing could feel very wrong. Actually, this shouldn't be necessary here. He should have been able to ask Anna to find a solution together against Ahrend. But he couldn't ask her. She was completely closed off. No wonder, since she surely saw no way out but to play along with the perfidious game and thereby humiliate herself God knows how.

Mo shook his head. There had to be something. Something. And basically, he already knew what.

Already a few weeks previously, he had come across a file that he did not know how to classify. It was only noted with the title Grimm and was located on a hard drive that was not supposed to belong to the computer. Everything was confused and when he asked Anna about it, hoping to have something on Ahrend, she nervously refused.

"That's mine," she had said. "Please don't tell anyone. My computer's broken, and it's kind of easier to do my stuff here anyway."

He believed her. At least he pretended to believe her, and then he programmed a loophole on the computer to have access to the files, even if she had resecured it. Now he would take a closer look at the files.

It took a while until he had seen everything so far. When it was all spread out before him in black and white, he no longer knew what to think. He quickly scribbled some notes on a sheet of paper. When he was done, he looked at them again and still couldn't believe it.

No wonder Anna was afraid when Ahrend had to deal with something like that. But could that be the case? And how deep was Anna in this?

All of a sudden, Mo felt very queasy. This exceeded even his expectations, even if he could not yet make any sense of it. But he believed that he finally had enough pieces of the puzzle together for others to solve this. He would have liked to download the files or copy them to a stick, but this was refused. However, this did not matter. The notes he had made and the photos he took with his smartphone were enough. Now the only question was to whom he should hand over the information.

Hastily, he stood up and almost forgot to turn the computer off again. As he walked through the large room, he looked through the windows to see if he could spot anyone outside, but there was no one. But there was a feeling... Something wasn't right, quite apart from the actual thing he was on the trail of here.

When he stepped out of the store, the feeling did not subside. The street he was so familiar with, even in the dark, suddenly seemed very threatening.

He would have loved to call Ben. But Ben could do nothing, and Mo wanted to have his hands free now so he could be ready for anything.

Sergey appeared as if from nowhere. Fast, brutal, unstoppable. But Mo was prepared. Since childhood, his father had taught him to be able to defend himself, and Mo had continued to hone his skills. So he was not the helpless victim that the attacker – a rather skinny guy in whom Mo directly recognized a Russian ancestry – expected. Nevertheless, the man was still very fast and skillful.

Sergey reached for Mo, sure to hit him hard with his other hand. But Mo dodged, grabbed the hand that held him and twisted it. Mo heard a hiss that came from Sergey drawing air in between his teeth. Instinctively, Mo let his fist crash on the arm twisted in this way, and then turned and, still turning, punched at the attacker's face. But Sergey ducked under the blow, turned and struck Mo's right ribs with his free hand, forcing him to let go of Sergey's hand.

Sergey smiled, opened and closed his hand. "Not bad!" he declared in the broadest Russian accent, then casually stood up.

But as a skilled fighter, Mo immediately recognized that he had someone in front of him who certainly had some higher combat experience. "What do you want?" he hissed back at him. "I don't have any money."

Sergey raised his eyebrows in amazement. "You go into a bank at this hour and come out with no money?"

The pause gave Mo time to think. "And you, of all people, are lurking here at this hour?"

Sergey shrugged his shoulders. "Maybe I was lucky."

Mo shook his head. "You were expecting me."

Sergey smiled. But it was not an evil smile, but one full of appreciation. "You're a smart guy. Then you know what I want, too. Be smart and give it to me."

Mo's mind was working at full speed. *Who was this Ahrend cooperating with?*

Sergey nodded. "I guess that means no."

Again the assault resumed. Mo could still fend off the first blows, but the force of Sergey's punches and the hardness of his fists and arms were incredible. Already Mo thought he was hitting steel again and again and he had to grit his teeth.

Then Sergey's blows came through as well. They hit Mo's body like heavy iron balls and drove the air out of his lungs, while Mo already thought he could hear his bones cracking.

Nevertheless, his many hours of training came to his aid. He had never taken such blows there, and even the guys he usually had to deal with didn't come close to Sergey's skills, but Mo managed to land hits himself, which, however, had less effect than he hoped.

Sergey seemed to be able to take a lot of punishment. He received two direct hits to his head, which had no effect.

Mo, on the other hand, had the impression that his fist had hit a concrete wall.

This time, however, he did not wait and immediately went on the attack. He tried to get through Sergey's defenses to land more blows. He would only be able to fight this opponent with stamina. He would have to wear him down blow by blow and not let up. He had already learned this from his father: someone who had decided to attack you had already crossed the greatest possible line for him and would not let up. On the contrary. Resistance would increase his brutality and determination. You had to eliminate someone like that and make sure that he could no longer be a danger to you.

Mo hit and hit, using all his skills. He had already been involved in many a brawl as a youth, was a hothead and even aggressively sought out fights. That it had been Ben, of all people, who finally got him away from that had something very ironic about it. But that was the way life played out.

Mo punched and kicked, used his elbows, as well as his knees. Again and again he managed to break through his opponent's guard and land hard hits.

But Sergey also fought back and his blows were paying off, wearing down his opponent.

Mo had never felt such pain in a fight. He could take it, but Sergey's blows were of a kind as if he were beating Mo with an iron bar.

Mo heard his bones crack, probably even one or two ribs were broken. He gritted his teeth, remembered his anger and drew strength from it. Now he brutally beat Sergey. Blow by blow he drove him back. Blocked his attacks. Broke through his guard. And let his fist crash into his face again and again.

Finally, Sergey sank down, covered in blood, propping himself up on his hands, while Mo stood over him, breathing heavily and with his fists raised, waiting for his opponent to make even one wrong move.

Sergey squatted on his lower legs and laughed at Mo. "You have spirit!"

Before Mo realized it, Sergey was already hurling a knife at him. The blade penetrated deep into his leg. Before he could scream, Sergey was already on him, punching him again and again with full force. He didn't know what was keeping him on his feet. When Mo struck at Sergey with more desperation than coordination, Sergey hardly made an effort to dodge. Instead, he suddenly held another knife in his hand and rammed it twice into Mo's body.

"You fought well, but now it's over," Sergey only said, sounding as if he was talking to a friend whose lost battle he regretted.

Almost carefully, he supported Mo as he slumped to the ground. Mo watched helplessly as Sergey put the knife away and searched Mo's pockets, finally taking out his wallet, smartphone and the piece of paper with the list. Sergey took a closer look at the list and frowned.

"What is this gibberish? A code?"

Mo smiled, showing his bloody teeth.

Sergey nodded appreciatively. "You're full of surprises." With that, he squatted down next to Mo and held the list in front of his face. "What does it say?"

Mo coughed. "The rating for your mother on Whore Portal."

Sergey's eyes flashed. It was only a brief moment, but Mo had noticed it after

all. "I'll give you..."

Sergey did not get any further.

Mo pulled the knife out of his leg and rammed it into Sergey's body. Sergey had seen the movement, but could not react quickly enough.

Sergey rolled to the side and Mo mobilized all his strength to push himself to his feet. With brute force of will, he kicked Sergey's head and hit him on the forehead, sending his head flying to the side.

Mo quickly grabbed his smartphone and the list and stumbled back. The pain in his body was hellish, but he couldn't give up now.

No retreat. No giving up.

Stumbling more than anything else, Mo tried to reach his car as fast as he could. His leg wanted to give way, his head just fainted, his heart could barely do its job, but Mo fought it.

Mo had always grumbled about the new electronics in the cars. "Who needs that? They really teach you to be lazy," he had always said. But here and now, he was glad that he didn't have to do anything but approach his car and touch the door handle. Immediately, the door opened. The car's electronics recognized the key, which was still in Mo's pocket.

As soon as he had struggled into the driver's seat, he would have preferred to rest first. But that wasn't possible, of course. He couldn't stay here. He had to leave.

Again and again he felt as if he was going to black out, but he fought against it. He felt so weak. So weak. And this pain... He felt his life leaving him through the two wounds. Sergey had twisted the blade on both thrusts as he pulled back, so these wounds would not close on their own. If he didn't see a doctor as soon as possible, he was doomed.

Just rest a little, his head tried to coax him. *Just a little bit...*

Mo saw Sergey stirring. Immediately he gritted his teeth, pushed the clutch through and pressed the starter button. The engine roared and Mo put the car in reverse. Through the window, he could still see Sergey getting to his feet. He would have preferred to just drive over him, but then changed his mind.

By the time Sergey had fully risen and pulled the knife from his side, Mo was already at the end of the street.

With his face contorted in pain, Sergey took out his cell phone. It clicked after the first ring.

"He got away," was all he communicated. On the other end of the line, he thought he heard a snort. Then a click sounded and the line went dead.

4

It was cold.

It was always cold in the woods, but the boys had gotten used to that. They had lived here since they were born, or could not remember ever living anywhere else. If they had lived anywhere else, no one talked about it. There was only the now. And the future. They were only to learn from the past of others how to behave now and in the future. What their task was. Their sacred task with which they had been entrusted. All of them. And they were not to fail in fulfilling it.

They were still too young to fulfill their ultimate task. But they would be prepared for it, so that they would once be the men they already were deep inside. This was to begin today. The day they had all been waiting for – Finn, Erik, Matt, Gunnar and the others.

Early in the morning they had been roused from their beds with loud words. The rain pelted the communal shelter in an incessant barrage, drenching each and every one of them as they stood in rows, trembling, fearful, but also full of anticipation. The time had finally come.

Although the voices speaking to them were loud, they were barely audible through the incessant rain. But it didn't matter, because they all had to do the same thing.

They ran across the forest. Always one after the other. Ran and ran. None of them dared to give up, whine or show greater weakness. Weakness was not tolerated. As a member of the community, one did not show weakness. Weakness was a characteristic of others. Those who had to be defeated. That was what they were trained to do. They would not be weak.

No retreat. No surrender. No mercy.

Again and again, this was drilled into them. Even now, when they were running to exhaustion to comply again and again, these words echoed through their heads, so that they never forgot them. The mantra of the warriors.

Once they would belong. To the chosen ones. The warriors. Who would redeem their battered people and lead them back to their old strength.

And he would be one of them.

Ben stood in front of the mirror, his hands resting on the sink, and looked himself in the eyes. Those brown eyes. Dark. Almost as dark as his black hair. Black. Like his soul.

He closed his eyes. But there were those images again. They waited in the darkness and in his thoughts. And in the blackness of the ink of his tattoo.

Slowly he opened his eyes again and looked at his reflection.

"You have to accept yourself," Mo's father had said.

"But I'm a monster," he heard his own, then much more youthful voice say. The images haunted him again and again. He just couldn't get rid of them.

Not as a teenager and not now. He only had to close his eyes and they were there, haunting him in his dreams.

There were tablets that ensured a dreamless sleep, but that was not good in the long run. So Ben had done without the pills as well as he could, turned to other methods or simply ran around sleepless and...

He shook his head.

"But I'm a monster." Against his youthful self.

He was barely sixteen years old when Ben came into Mo's family. Why his father took him in, Ben could not explain. Didn't he have the mark on his body that made it unmistakably clear that he was nothing but a monster in human form?

The sign.

The symbol.

The one and so many more. The one on his arm that showed he was.... Again the images were there. The screams. Despair.

"You deserve it!"

The big man. Bald. Beard. That bushy beard. Like a Viking. All.

He literally felt the leather straps that held him and felt the pain of the needle that was incessantly penetrating the skin, turning it black.

Ben took a breath and looked in the mirror again. Finally, he grabbed the hem of his black T-shirt and pulled it over his head. Now his upper body was free and he looked at the symbol emblazoned on the left side of his chest. The symbol that branded him for what he was.

"No matter where you go," Odin had said in his mind, "this will always remind you of who you are. And everyone can see who you are."

Ben let his fingers slide over the wide bars of the tattoo and then looked at the inside of his left forearm, which showed a detailed skull. A skull provided with runes. Insiders knew what it stood for. Mo's father had known it too. He knew what symbol adorned Ben's chest. What symbol was on his left forearm. Knew its meaning. And yet...

Ben didn't understand it until today. Mo's father didn't have to do that. No one had obligated him to do so, and on the other hand, everything had already been settled. But Mo's father had insisted on taking the boy home with so much anger, but also despair in him. The boy, this ticking time bomb, who held an incalculable potential for danger. And yet Mo's father had gone along with it. Of his own accord.

Ben took a breath and put the shirt back on. He would never understand why Mo's father had done this. But he would always be grateful to him. He had seen something in him that no one had seen before and that he himself had not thought possible.

Mo had seen it too. Not at first, but later. They each shared a rage, an anger that exceeded any expression of their surroundings. Before Ben joined them, Mo must have thought he was the angriest boy in his neighborhood, maybe even the city. Ben proved him wrong. And yet it had been Ben who cured Mo of his constant outbursts of anger. He, of all people, was the boy with the broad swastika on his chest.

Mo's father had offered to have it removed. But Ben didn't want that. It belonged to him and should remind him of who he was and where he came from. It was part of his identity.

He knew himself that this was strange, but they respected his wish, even if it meant that he had to explain himself every time he took off his shirt.

This is exactly what should be achieved.

He was not safe anywhere. Always a leper. Everyone saw who he was. And he would be hunted.

56

And he would have to decide. When would he let his demon out? Eventually, the time would come.

Ben immediately saw that something was wrong when Mo got out of the car. He could see that he was bleeding profusely, even though it was deepest night outside. Without hesitation, he ran outside and caught Mo before he fell down.

"In!" Mo breathed weakly, and Ben put his arm around his shoulder, dragging his friend into the house like a wounded soldier in a horrific war.

They had barely entered the apartment when Mo collapsed, powerless. Ben closed the door and dragged Mo into the living room. He didn't care that he was bleeding all over the place.

Gently, he lowered him to the couch, then searched for the cause of Mo's blood loss, but Mo held his hand tightly.

"No time," he breathed. "They must be after me. But I had to come, had to come..."

Ben frowned at him, uncomprehending. "You need a doctor."

Mo smiled and shook his head. Then, painfully, he pulled out the piece of paper with the list and pressed it into Ben's hand.

Ben looked at it in disbelief and Mo smiled again.

"You have to take care of her. Take care of Anna. Promise me that. That you'll take care of her."

Ben took a deep breath and exhaled. "We have to call the police."

Mo shook his head decisively. "No. No police. You have to handle this. Protect Anna and get Ahrend.

Promise me you won't let him get away with it and make him pay. That you'll make everyone pay..."

"I... " Ben started, but fell silent when Mo grabbed him by the arm. His eyes were full of anger.

"I know who you are. Don't tell me you can't. I know what you've done. I know what you do. That you're the one beating the shit out of all these rightwing assholes. And that you can do a lot more." Mo coughed and Ben didn't argue, letting him talk. "I'm your brother. And I know about the anger that's in you. I know what's been done to you. But I also know you can kick all their asses."

Ben looked deeply into Mo's eyes. "I don't remember."

Mo gritted his teeth. "Bullshit. You've got to take care of Anna. They'll be after her."

"You?"

Mo nodded weakly and closed his eyes. "Some shit is going down. Something even nastier than I thought. Ahrend's into some real big shit. The guy who mugged me, that wasn't a street thug. He was a professional. The police can't protect Anna against someone like that. And Anna won't be safe until Ahrend has been stopped and all his people have been dealt with. Do you understand?"

Ben was silent for a moment. "You're wrong about me."

Mo smiled wearily. "For your sake, I wish it were so. But for Anna's sake, I wish I wasn't wrong." Then Mo suddenly stopped and his eyes fixed on the door, spellbound. "Shit!"

The next moment the door flew open and three men dressed in black came rushing in. Before Ben even understood what was happening to him, one of the men kicked him in the head. He was thrown to the side and remained dazed on the floor. Immediately another man came and kicked him repeatedly until he stopped moving.

The men paid no further attention to him. While one began to trash the room, the other went to the other rooms, while the third stood in front of Mo and looked down on him.

"You have something that belongs to us."

Mo breathed heavily and looked up at the man, whose deadpan expression showed incredible harshness and whose accent suggested even more Russian origin than that of the attacker at the bank.

"You're going to regret this," Mo stated, pulling out his smartphone.

The man shook his head. "I don't think so. Rather, you regret ever sticking your nose into someone else's business."

Mo smiled a bloody smile. "For one thing, I'm a banker. Other people's affairs are my affairs. And then I'm a German Turk. It's a terrible mixture, because I feel I'm affected by everything."

The man smiled and put his hands over each other, so that Mo could see blue tattoos there, which told him directly that this man belonged to the Russian mafia. Probably a member of a brutal squad that was responsible for the rough stuff.

All at once the man kicked Mo's belly right on the wound. Mo cried out. "Another stupid line, fucking Arab?" the man hissed.

Mo was breathing heavily. "What the hell are you waiting for?" he hissed through clenched teeth. "What the hell are you waiting for?"

The man looked amused. "What am I waiting for? You mean why don't I kill you? Because I like to admire Sergey's work. He's an artist and you're a dead man. So I'm just waiting for you to die here, Arab."

Mo smiled. "Who said I was talking to you?"

The man looked at Mo in confusion. Then he noticed a movement next to him. Turning his head, he just had time to see that Ben was no longer lying on the floor.

Before he could move, Ben hit him in the ears with the palms of his hands with full force, causing the man's eardrums to burst. The Russian cried out and Ben rammed his fist into his face. The very next moment he rammed his fist into his solar plexus. The man gasped for air and went down on his knees.

The other Russian, who had been busy trashing the room, came rushing in. He pulled out a knife to stab Ben. However, Ben dodged the knife and was able to escape the next attack. When the Russian stabbed again, Ben quickly grabbed a floor lamp, parried the stab with it, and then let the base of the lamp crash against the Russian's knee. The Russian cried out, but still lunged again with the knife. But he could not catch him. Ben again let the foot of the lamp crash against the knee, and then directed it against the attacker's hand. The attacker let go of the knife and finally went down.

There was no time for Ben to take a breath. The third Russian came back from the bedroom. When he saw that his two comrades were lying on the floor, he immediately drew his pistol. Holding the pistol with both hands, he searched the room.

Suddenly a book came flying at him and hit him right in the head. The next moment Ben jumped on him, not only knocking his gun aside, but also ramming his knee into his torso below the chest. The man gasped for air, but managed to hold on. He hit Ben, who took the blow and staggered back briefly. The very next moment, however, he had caught himself again and went on the attack. Ben parried the Russian's attacks and then covered him with punch combinations that did not miss. Ben struck at every spot that offered him a target. He struck with incredible hardness, fed by a deep rage that gave him strength. Again and again his fist crashed into the face of his opponent, until he finally went down, bleeding heavily.

Ben exhaled and looked in disbelief at the devastation all around him. But then he remembered Mo and ran to his friend.

Mo smiled, but seemed even weaker than before. "Father was right. It's in you. Or you've been practicing hard."

Ben shook his head. "Don't talk. We need to get a doctor."

Mo shook his head resolutely, even though it cost him a lot of strength. "No, you have to protect Anna. They're probably after her by now." With that, he pointed to the smartphone and finally took out the note.

"Take this and get out of here. You don't have much time."

Ben seemed torn. "Mo..."

Mo shook his head again. "You're the only one I trust. Sonnenallee 38. Apartment building. Light blue paint. Second floor."

Ben was about to say something else when Mo's eyes suddenly widened and he almost jumped up. In the next moment he pushed Ben aside before he himself was shaken by bullets.

In his shock, Ben's body reacted as if by itself. With a jump he brought himself out of the danger zone. But the last Russian, whom he had sent to the ground but had now recovered, was waiting there. He took out a knife, but Ben was faster. Before the man knew it, Ben had pelted him with blows and twisted his wrist so that the blade was now pointing at the man himself. As Ben swept his legs away, the Russian fell onto his own blade, which bored into his skull below his eye.

All this had lasted only a fraction of a second. In the next moment, bullets whizzed past Ben. If the shooter hadn't been injured, Ben was sure, he would have put him down long ago.

When he heard the *click*, Ben didn't hesitate and went straight into the attack. Like a tiger, he leapt at the leader, whose eyes widened in horror. Before Ben hit him, however, the other Russian attacked him from the side, threw him to the ground and punched him, but couldn't land any real hits from his position.

Ben wriggled out from under his arms, grabbed his right arm and twisted it so hard that it finally broke. The man cried out and Ben hit him again and again in the larynx. Gasping and rolling his eyes, the man went to the ground where he finally lay twitching.

Ben immediately turned to the last opponent. He had finally reloaded and raised his pistol. But Ben lunged forward and hit the gun before the Russian could fire it. The man didn't even know what happened to him as Ben's well-aimed blows rained down on him, seeming to splinter bone at every point, until Ben finally wrestled the pistol from him and was now pointing it at him.

The man looked at Ben in amazement and saw only Ben's emotionless face.

"I..." the man began. That's as far as he got, because Ben shot him in both shoulders, then in the arms, and finally in both kneecaps. Screaming, the man slumped to the ground, where he simply collapsed like a wet sack and whimpered.

Ben turned to Mo, who was sitting on the sofa with open but empty eyes, still holding the smartphone and the note. Powerless, Ben stood in front of him and paused for a moment until he finally realized that his best friend had taken his last breath. Ben gently stroked Mo's eyelids with his hand, as he could no longer bear the sight of the expressionless frozen pupils. As he did so, he closed his own eyes and his face contorted in anger.

When he opened them again, they were moist with tears. Taking a deep breath, he crouched down in front of Mo and took the cell phone and the note from him.

Ben heard a rasping laugh and looked to the last Russian still alive.

"We will make you pay," this one announced. "You and that bitch. We're going to fuck you both. We're going to give you the worst of the worst for free. We..."

Ben shot him in the stomach and the man groaned.

"You're not going to do anything but die in pain," was all Ben said. He would have liked to say and do more, but then he heard a noise. Voices. Reinforcements for the Russians had arrived.

He quickly grabbed one of the knives and left the room through the patio door. The very next moment, more men entered Mo's apartment, this time directly with drawn weapons.

"Garden!" breathed the remaining man and immediately three men went through the patio door into the garden. However, the garden was pitch black, so that they could not see anything. Ben had disappeared.

5

Russev hated bad news. During his time in the army, he had constantly received bad news. His main task as an officer had been not to let this bad news get him down and to make the best of it. It had always been a matter of perspective and how to make a virtue out of necessity. Moreover, his time in the army had helped him with his current business and it would not have been conceivable without it.

Russev had always thought that there was much money to be made especially in a country that had nothing. In Russia, there was always a need for weapons, drugs, and women to do with as they pleased. But Russev was astonished to find that the need was even greater in countries that had much more.

Russev had left the old homeland years ago and never regretted it. Some- times he felt a little homesick, but he would never set foot on Russian soil again. He owed a lot to Russia and the conditions that prevailed there. But he would never forget the miserable winters. The cold. The harshness. And the hopelessness. That there was nothing and everyone was just trying to survive as best they could. All the lies.

Here, everything was different. And yet everything he had built up was now threatened.

Russev stroked his right hand over his face, which was already far too greasy for his liking. Actually, he had wanted to spend a nice evening with a bottle of wine and his wife. He had succeeded in doing so, but then his smartphone had rung and the nice evening had ended.

When it rang again, he knew it couldn't be good news.

"Did you get him?" he asked.

"The Turk is lying here, dead," came the curt reply. "But his smartphone is missing. Yuri says there was a second man. Not a Turk. According to his ID, a Ben Becker. Also works at the bank."

Russev snorted. "You got him?"

The man on the other end of the line hesitated. "No. He took out Yuri and the others."

"Took them out?"

"Yuri's still alive, but I'm sure he won't make it. The other two are dead."

Again Russev snorted. He had known that the whole thing would become a problem as soon as he found out about it. He had tolerated it at first, but when there were the first signs that it could all blow up, he had wanted to end it. Now it was too late and he had to deal with this mess.

"Find this Ben Becker guy. Get the smartphone and whatever else he's carrying."

With that, he hung up. He felt like a vodka, but that was never good. He needed to be awake and lucid.

One of the problems of his home country was that there was too much alcohol and too much drinking. People never made good decisions there. Russev had always appreciated vodka as something that warmed him up on the cold nights. But he had never drunk too much, and never on duty. That's probably why he still had his business, which he had been building up until the present day. But now everything was threatening to blow up and he was forced to attract more attention than he had ever done and was comfortable with.

The smartphone rang again. An unlisted number. Sullenly, Russev picked it up. "What do you want?"

"Keep your men out of this," the Administrator's disguised voice rang out.

Russev laughed mirthlessly. "Or what? Are you going to have me whacked? By Sergey? Or one of your other killers?"

"Keep your men out of this," the Administrator repeated. "I'll take care of it."

Again Russev laughed. "That's exactly why I had to put my men in, because you misjudged that stupid Turk. And now, not only is your business in danger of being blown, but mine is as well. And probably everyone's. Do you think I or the others will stand by and do nothing?"

The Administrator was silent.

Russev smiled, then continued, "We've been watching you for quite a while and tolerating what you've been doing. But now you are endangering all of us. And we're not going to let that happen."

"Your men are attracting too much attention!" the Administrator objected.

"Maybe they wouldn't have to if you hadn't misjudged that Turk so much. Besides, you overlooked his friend, Ben Becker, who took out three of my men and is now gone with the important information. But my men know where to look. The Turk has always been in close contact with this Anna. Apparently, he sent this Becker guy to protect her."

Silence again. "I'll look into it."

Russev snorted. "You had your chance to straighten everything out. But you failed. Sergey was too sure. That's up to you. I'll have a word with him and go back to taking care of all his affairs."

"Don't get in my way."

Russev grinned. "Or what? You think I'm still afraid of you after the way you've screwed everything up? I'd suggest you get the hell out of here and let the professionals do the work."

The Administrator was silent for a moment before continuing. "You've been warned."

Russev's face turned red. "You're warning *me?!* I'm going to..."

The Administrator had hung up. Russev slammed the smartphone down on the table, then laughed. The Administrator would pay for that. But all in good time. What happened in the next few hours was going to be crucial. He was not yet ready to give up his life here and leave. He liked it here. And as long as there was still a chance that he could avert everything, he would do so. But some things would have to change.

No sooner had the Administrator interrupted the conversation to Russev than he sent the SMS he had prepared for this eventuality, which had unfortunately occurred. The recipients who received them knew exactly what to do and would take appropriate steps.

Now he could only hope that everything would turn out well.

6

Finn heard the dogs again as he searched his way through the dark forest. He had to get to the river, because only there would they lose his scent.

The dogs. They were huge. He had seen them. In their kennels. Had seen them maul alive other dogs that were thrown to them. Heard the pitiful sounds of the dying animals, overwhelmed with such brute force, whimpering, whining, and brutally slaughtered.

Again and again he had been forced to watch this. And now the dogs were after him.

"You get a head start," Odin had told them. As always, without a movement in his face, but with those dark eyes that were as intimidating as anything in the world. "If you apply everything you've been taught, you'll be fine. If not... it's not worth talking about." Then he leaned in very close to each of their faces. "You know: no backing down. No giving up. No mercy."

Those words had been directed not only at Finn, but at the other boys, all of whom were of a similar age to Finn. Some of them, like Erik, Gunnar, and Matt, already had such a hard look on their faces, not inferior to that of Odin. Others showed some excitement, some even fear.

Finn had shown no fear. Fear was a weakness that could not be afforded in this world. Only the youth who courageously went forward, his goal in his eye, could exist. Action should determine one's own actions. It had to get into one's body and soul, so that at the decisive moment one took action, was quick and no longer had to think. They had been trained for this. They had sharpened their senses and their instincts, reactions. Acting with the greatest possible effectiveness in order to be able to serve their community one day.

The barking came closer and closer. From somewhere he heard shrieks of pain. The dogs had caught one of them. The dogs would not let go of him until the order was given. If it was given.

Finn had seen for himself how a boy of the community had been mauled by the dogs, and Odin had stood by and watched the whole thing without emotion. Unworthy ones were simply buried, somewhere in the forest. Not deep, so that the wild boars would do the actual dirty work and make the carcass disappear.

Again, the barking. The river was close – Finn could smell it already. He clasped his knife with a firm grip. He had known this time would come and had sharpened the blade daily. It was a good knife, stainless steel, hardened in the blood of his birth. The blade was 8 inches long and nearly 2 inches wide. Finn had customized the handle himself so that it fit his hand perfectly. He had also fitted the knife with a short leather strap that he had tied around his wrist so he could not lose the knife so easily, even if it should slip out of his hand.

During his escape, he had cut off a branch that seemed particularly straight and stable. With it he had left a hint to his pursuers in which direction he had run, but they would have had no trouble to find out.

While running, he had freed the branch of everything superfluous and finally sharpened it as if he wanted to ram it into the body of a vampire. In addition, he had really made himself a couple of stakes, which he attached to his belt.

A brief second in the mud had to be enough to camouflage him. Already at the beginning he had parted with a shirt that hindered him more than it helped. What was important were good boots, sturdy pants and a belt. A shirt could only serve the enemy to hold you down.

The mud stuck to Finn's body. It was chilly, but he didn't care. He could warm himself when he was safe and he had survived the test. That was all that mattered.

The river. Only a few more yards.

Again a scream was heard. Klaas. Even though Finn couldn't swear to it, he was sure it was Klaas whose wailing, pain-distorted scream he heard.

He closed his eyes for a moment, then kept running. He couldn't help Klaas. Certainly not now.

There was the river. He had made it. Here the dogs could only lose his trail. No nose was so good that it could have made him out in the flowing water.

The barking came closer and Finn felt a chill run down his spine. Fenrir. He was the biggest and meanest of the beasts. That he took part in this agitation was actually already too violent.

Fenrir was the embodiment of brutality and hopelessness. Straight from hell, yet merely the product of a breeding that had begun decades, if not centuries ago. His ancestors had already hunted down and mauled to death escaped slaves on plantations. Or had engaged in brutal battles against the so-called savages, the sub-humans, to tear out their guts for the pleasure of the spectators.

No one who fell into Fenrir's clutches would ever survive this. Unless his lord and master Odin ordered him to retreat. But that would never happen.

Fenrir was behind him. Not much longer and he would pounce on him too, sink his teeth into his body and drain the life out of him...

All at once Finn believed that at least this hound from hell, this pitch-black beast with yellow eyes and ivory-white teeth as long as his fingers, could smell him in the water. He gripped the handle of his knife tighter, as well as his spear, and ran. Only a short distance and he would have made it.

Suddenly something rammed him in the side and pulled him to the ground. He thought he felt Fenrir's teeth in his flesh, but there was nothing. Just the absorbing pain of the impact on his shoulder.

Immediately Finn tried to push aside the weight that was on him, but something, or rather someone, forced his hands down.

"I knew you'd go that way!" Gunther's unmistakable voice. "You're so predictable. Relying on familiar things and always choosing the same routes. If you really had the abilities Odin sees in you, you could find your way anywhere and wouldn't have to keep seeking the protection of the known."

Gunther pressed Finn's arms to the ground and grinned from his weasel-like face. He was two years older than Finn, taller, more muscular. In fact, he should have passed the test long ago, but a leg injury had prevented that. An injury that Finn had inflicted on him. Gunther had never forgiven him for that, and now he would take revenge.

"Get off me!" Finn shouted, trying to brace himself against Gunther's forces, but to no avail. No one of Gunther's vintage had ever defeated him. Even elders feared him, for he was a brutal, ruthless fighter and thus exactly what the community wanted. Gunther loved to torture his opponents and intentionally inflict injuries on them, even if they were actually his comrades.

"Get off me!" Finn repeated. "Fenrir is right here!"

Gunther grinned maliciously. "I know."

"He'll kill us both!"

Gunther's eyes glinted with malice. "No – just you, little maggot!"

Finn looked at him aghast, and Gunther gloated.

"I should have been the leader one day. Me alone. Everyone knew that. Odin saw it in me. And I did all I could to prove myself worthy of it." Gunther's grip tightened as he continued through clenched teeth. "But then you, little maggot, came along and spoiled everything. Refused to give up like the others. And smashed my kneecap with a rock, a fucking rock. A rock! My knee and my hand. Smashed. And Odin turned away from me. Everyone turned away. I would never be one of the warriors with these injuries. Never be a leader. Everyone knew that. I was only tolerated. Tolerated! No matter how well I still fight, I'm just a cripple to them."

Gunther paused for a moment and listened before turning back to Finn. "And Odin watched you from then on. Oh, I have seen the way he looks at you. That's exactly how he once looked at me. You took everything from me. And for that you will now die!"

With that, Gunther stood up and took out a vial, the contents of which he spread over Finn before closing it again.

"Do you know what this is? This is what they sprinkle on Fenrir's victims, because it makes him furious. Just a few drops is enough and he goes wild. Then he won't even listen to Odin. I have stolen a vial and waited especially for this moment. I'm going to enjoy watching Fenrir tear you apart right before my eyes."

Finn looked at Gunther, then at the vial. Finally, he turned his head toward the barking that was getting closer. Looking across the river, he could make out Erik and Matt some distance away, transfixed as they watched what was happening. From them, however, no help was to be expected. Just to save him, they would not mess with Gunther or Fenrir. He was on his own.

Do not think! Know! Act!

Finn jumped up, grabbed his spear and knocked the vial out of Gunther's hand. Deftly he caught it, only to open it immediately and empty the contents completely on Gunther.

"What are you doing?!" Gunther cried out in panic.

Both looked in the same direction at the same time and saw the black beast hurtling towards them. Gunther turned around and wanted to sprint towards the river. Finn, however, brought his spear around and crashed it against Gunther's knee, the one he had already injured. While Gunther slumped to the ground screaming, Finn sprinted off and jumped into the river at the very moment Fenrir lunged at the still screaming Gunther. Even underwater, Finn could still hear Fenrir's greedy noises and Gunther's shrill screams.

7

Ben was running. He didn't know when he had last run like this. Actually, he did, because the images came back, forced themselves into his consciousness, now of all times.

Ben could still hear Gunther's screams. Even now, when he was rushing through the woods. Why did the memories come back now of all times? Pushed themselves into his mind.

He tried to shake them off. If he wanted to escape his pursuers, he needed all his senses and concentration. Images from the past had no place here.

Not thinking! Know! Act!

It was not dogs that pursued Ben, but people. People made of flesh and blood. Of bone, muscle and sinew. Fragile. Vulnerable.

He had to protect Anna, that was all that mattered now.

No retreat. No giving up. No mercy.

His heart was beating up to his neck. Even more than when he had witnessed the whole event and finally saw how Fenrir gleefully mauled Gunther. Played with his prey and feasted on their desperate death struggle, as he had been taught.

Anger rose in Ben. The old familiar rage. Immeasurable. Uncontrollable. Now that Mo was dead.

He took a breath and slipped behind a tree. He had to get to Anna, but that way his pursuers would catch up with him first, or he'd lead them right to her. Neither was an option.

Making his way behind the tree, Ben tried to get his bearings. He could only estimate the number of his pursuers. Five? Maybe more. And they had spread out. One was coming right at him. Good.

The man held an automatic in his hand. The way he did it clearly showed Ben that this one was familiar with handling a gun, and he certainly would have no problem just shooting Ben.

Military training? Possibly. There were so many former soldiers from the East who were only too happy to be hired by criminal organizations. In most cases, these organizations also consisted purely of former or still-affiliated members of some military unit. The transitions were fluid and the connections were always maintained.

The man came closer and closer and Ben clasped his knife. As the man passed him, Ben jumped out of his hiding place in a flash, pushed the gun aside and rammed the blade up under his ribcage into his lungs, which immediately collapsed, making it impossible for him to scream.

Carefully, Ben lowered him to the ground and hid him behind the tree. Only then did he look at his face and take a breath. He had killed him. Just like that. He had assessed the danger situation in a split second and weighed the options. Another possibility would have been to take him out by an unarmed attack. But that would have taken too long and would have been too conspicuous, especially since it would have given the man the opportunity to draw attention to himself. Thus his death had been the only possibility. Besides...

Ben breathed in. He had truly killed the man without hesitation. The decision seemed logical to him. He didn't even have to think much about it, he had just done it, automatically. His movements had been perfect and the man had had no chance.

You are better than him.

A crack snapped Ben out of his thoughts. Immediately he ducked down and scanned the dead man's pockets with lightning speed. There he found another knife, brass knuckles, and several magazines to go with his automatic. He took everything and oriented himself to his further pursuer.

When he passed by, Ben grabbed him by the head, kicked his knee and slammed him against the tree with full force. Hammered his face against it so many times until the man stopped moving.

Out of nowhere, another man appeared. Ben gave him no chance to raise his pistol. Instinctively, he threw the knife at his neck and then shot him right between the eyes. While the man fell to the ground, Ben hid behind a tree in a flash and crouched down. As he had expected, two men came running and screaming. While they stood over the bodies of their dead comrades, still wondering what had happened, Ben came out from behind the tree and shot both of them in the head at close range.

He took a breath and looked around, listening. The only sounds he heard came from some distance away. As he bent down to the bodies and searched their pockets for magazines, he kept an eye out and his ears open for more enemies. But there was no one left.

Ben knew Sonnenallee. When they were younger, this was the neighborhood that had once been considered the better one. This is where people wanted to live, to raise their children in a quiet neighborhood. Here everything was clean, tidy, perfect. So perfect that some people made fun of it. Secretly, however, one wanted to live here only too gladly, where one could step out in the evening without problems before the door. Here, the neighbors invited each other to barbecue parties and didn't try to set your car on fire.

Mo and his family hadn't exactly lived in the worst neighborhood, but they hadn't lived in Sonnenallee either. Ben hadn't cared about that. He had never expected to ever be taken into such a home as Mo's family home. For him it had been paradise and Sonnenallee had been aspirational only because he wished it better for his adopted family, or whatever they were. No, wished for the best. They deserved the best.

Instead, Mo's father died as a result of injuries inflicted on him by a couple of teenage half-breeds because he tried to stop them from beating a boy to death. And Mo was now dead, too. Murdered by some gangsters who apparently wanted to prevent Mo from bringing to light what Ahrend was involved in. And of course, Mo was right when he assumed that Anna was also in danger.

Ben had not been able to save Mo because he had hesitated too long. But he would save Anna. Come what may.

No retreat. No giving up. No mercy.

He watched the house and let his eyes glide over the area. Every car, every tree, every house was scrutinized by him before he moved on. He took advantage of every cover he could find without pausing in his movement. Instinctively, he took advantage of the conditions of the environment. His senses were all heightened.

You have to be invisible. The less they see of you, the less they can judge you. The days of open combat are over. Warriors operate in the shadows.

Although he couldn't spot anyone, Ben crept around to the back of the building to the basement entrance that led to the garden. There were plenty of hiding places here that offered potential attackers protection from being discovered by him. Ben, however, could not discover anything.

Silently, he reached the cellar door, which was of course locked. He took out one of the knives, which was a military-style simple double-edged blade. Without thinking about what he had to do, Ben slid the blade between the door frame and the door. With a soft click, it opened and he slipped inside.

He looked for something to put in front of the door since he couldn't close it. He pushed a small shelf, on which old paint cans and cachepots were stowed, in front of it and placed some buckets and brooms crosswise, which served him as an alarm system. Should anyone use the same entrance, this would not go unnoticed by him.

Use your environment. Everything can be useful. Every object is a weapon.

Ben put the knife away again and gripped the handle of his pistol, which was equipped with a silencer. He would have preferred another weapon, but here he had to be ready to react quickly to take out several enemies as effectively as possible.

As he entered the stairwell, the lights immediately came on. Motion detectors. Ben pressed himself against the wall, but nothing happened.

The stairwell was simply white. Everything was clean. The floor was not slippery and one could see from the basement to the top floor. Hiding would be so difficult, for him, but also for his opponents.

When he passed the front door, he did so with extreme caution. There was no indication that anyone had tampered with it, nor that anyone was nearby.

He crept up to the second floor, where there were only two apartment doors. The sign on the doorbell was small and made of brass, the letters barely legible, but Ben recognized the name.

He considered ringing the bell or breaking in, but then decided to push the button. The sound wasn't loud, but to Ben's ears, any noise was one too many. He had no choice, however, and had to take a chance.

If he had broken down the door, there was a chance that Anna might have mistaken him for a burglar or even a hired thug. The way Mo had explained Anna's situation, Ben assumed that the young woman was expecting an unwelcome visitor. If she had any idea who Ahrend had gotten involved with, she knew that these people weren't exactly subtle.

He rang the doorbell again and stood clearly visible in front of the peephole. He had only met Anna once before, but he hoped that Mo had written him down so that Anna wouldn't call the police if she saw him standing in front of her door.

Ben listened and heard footsteps. Only softly, but clearly audible to him. He resisted the impulse to push the door open as soon as Anna opened it even a crack.

It would certainly have been easy for him to simply kick it in, since most of them had only a simple curtain lock, which would be useless in opposing a direct use of force.

Anna opened the door and Ben immediately recognized that it had considerably more than just a padlock. Around here, that could only mean that she was either paranoid or had realized what kind of guys she might be dealing with. Most likely, her windows were similarly secured. Good for her. But tonight that wouldn't be enough, since the men who were surely hunting her were more than just common burglars. Even a few more locks and the thickest security glass would not stop them.

Ben eyed Anna for a moment. She was wearing a gray tank top with a sports bra underneath along with red and black plaid pajama pants and white socks. Her hair was tied in a simple braid and her eyes looked as if she had slept through the night so far rather than really slept. It was probably not the first time this had happened today.

"Yes?" she asked hesitantly. "Ben? Am I right? Ben Becker? What are you doing here? Is something going on with Mo?"

Yes. It was something with Mo, but how could he explain it to her so directly here and now?

Yes, it's something with Mo. He's dead. But the blood on my hands and clothes is not his. And yes, he was shot, but it wasn't me, even though I have a gun.

That wouldn't sound very credible.

"You look terrible," Anna observed, and to Ben's great surprise, she opened the door. "What the hell happened to you?"

Ben considered lying. But that would damage the relationship of trust before it even existed.

"Mo was murdered," he said.

Anna looked at him, stunned. "What?!"

Then she slapped her hands over her mouth and her eyes wandered back and forth. Tears were forming and Ben could tell she was on the verge of a breakdown.

"May I come in, please?"

When Anna did not respond, he pushed his way into the apartment and closed the door.

Anna looked at him again, searching for answers in his face. "Why?"

Ben took a breath. He knew they didn't have much time, but he had to somehow get Anna to trust him and go with him. They weren't safe here.

He noticed Anna looking startled at his bloody hands, as well as the knife in his belt. He had tucked the gun into the back of his waistband.

"Is the blood his?" Anna asked in a trembling voice.

"Not all of it. But probably some."

Anna swallowed. "Did *you*...?"

Ben shook his head hastily. "No. He came back already badly hurt. I tried to stop the bleeding."

Anna nodded as if in a trance. "And the other blood?"

"Came from whoever was chasing him."

Anna swallowed. "What...? Why...? What were they chasing him for?"

Ben was silent for a moment. "He was at your computer in the branch because he thought he could find clues there about what Ahrend was blackmailing you with and what machinations he was involved in."

Anna was aghast. "At the branch office? But why?"

"Because he wanted to protect you. He believed Ahrend was taking advantage of you and..."

"... that he was harassing me," she added weakly. "Of course. That makes sense. I'm sure he believed that."

Ben pulled out the piece of paper and handed it to Anna. "Here, he wrote this down."

Carefully, Anna unfolded the note. The contents confused her even more. "This doesn't make any sense. It's just letters and numbers."

Ben nodded. "A code. It's how he used to encode notes he thought were important. With the right key, we can read it."

Anna frowned but slowly understood. "Do you have the key?"

Ben nodded. "Yes. But that doesn't matter right now. What matters is that he was worried about you when he died. He thought the men might be after you, too, and do something to you."

Anna looked at him in panic. "Me? But..." She nodded. "Because I know too much. Ahrend wants to kill me because I might know too much."

Ben nodded. "That's what it looks like. And his men are probably on their way here right now."

Anna looked around and began to pace apathetically up and down her small hallway. Suddenly she paused and seemed to think hard. "But Ahrend doesn't have any men. He's a banker."

"They were, as far as I could tell, Russians."

Anna seemed to realize. Then she nodded. "Russev."

"I beg your pardon?"

"Russev. Ahrend has connections to Russev. He's like the resident Russian mob boss here. I don't know if that's true. But it would fit. An unscrupulous businessman, involved in all kinds of illegal mafias, is probably a better description. But he actually keeps a low profile."

Ben took a breath. "Not today." Anna nodded, then looked around again in near panic.

"They'll come. I'm sure Ahrend told Russev to kill me." She slapped her hands in front of her face and looked back at Ben. "But why did Mo send you? Why didn't he call the police right away?"

Ben was silent for a moment. "He didn't believe the police could protect you. His father was a policeman and he always had a very definite opinion about what the police could do in a case like this. Besides, Mo probably believed you might be involved in everything. That Ahrend had something on you and the police might then discover it."

Anna leaned against the wall. All this was apparently too much for her. "But why you?"

Ben paused again for a moment. "He trusts me."

Anna snorted. "To be able to protect me? From the Russian mafia? You're a banker, for crying out loud!"

Ben couldn't help a brief smile. "That's what I told him."

"And yet he sends you."

Ben nodded. "Listen. We've got to get out of here. I'm your only chance to go underground right now. Put on something for moving well and, most importantly, running fast. And do it quickly. We've wasted way too much time already, but it's important that you believe me."

Anna smiled mirthlessly. "So I have no choice?"

Ben looked at her piercingly. "If you want to survive, no."

Anna nodded.

"Please give me back the note."

Anna looked at the paper and smiled sheepishly. "Excuse me."

She handed the note back to Ben and then disappeared into one of the rooms.

Ben looked around. The back of his neck prickled, and he had the feeling that someone would come storming through the apartment door or window any minute now. In addition, he somehow still felt the need to follow Anna. But she would surely have little understanding if he entered the room where she was changing. So he confined himself to listening carefully for any suspicious noises.

Carefully, he approached one of the large windows, which during the day in summer certainly let in a lot of light and made the pastel-colored apartment seem even brighter. He liked the apartment. There were not many objects, but a lot of empty space between the furniture. Everything was new, most of the white simple but tasteful. There were no photos, but paintings of beautiful landscapes.

Of course, all this was irrelevant, because all that mattered to him was that he discovered potential hiding places for attackers or for himself, weak points and objects that could be used as weapons. All this happened automatically, without Ben having to think about it for long, instinctively.

When he stepped up to the window and looked out, he didn't see how beautiful the location was either, only the strategic features. A large meadow the size of two soccer fields. A playground in the middle. Scattered trees at the edges. Behind it, the parking lot.

From here, it would be difficult to sneak up on them unnoticed. But if they had to get out, they would have an equally hard time. Then this played into the hands of possible attackers.

"Can you see anyone?" Anna wanted to know. She had put on athletic pants, sneakers, and a long-sleeve fleece jacket, over which she shouldered a small backpack, all dark. She tied a simple braid and appeared calmer than she had been a moment before.

Ben shook his head. "No. But that doesn't have to mean anything. Do you have any weapons?"

Anna looked at him indignantly. "I'm a bank clerk. My weapon is a laptop!"

Ben smiled wryly. "Any combat experience?"

"Zumba?"

Ben shrugged. "Might even be useful. But I meant something else."

Anna showed a pinched face. "Self-defense class for women. Had stopped once, but now started again."

"Better than nothing."

Anna was irritated. "Better than nothing? I thought it was good."

"How many men were in the classes?"

"Well, none. It was a self-defense course for women, after all."

"And you trained with them."

"Of course. I always signed up when asked to fight."

"With protective gear."

"What are you getting at?"

"Are you often attacked by women in protective gear who want to rape you?"

Anna was silent.

Ben looked at her penetratingly. "The men who come after you are not women in protective clothing. And once they meet you, you'll know what I'm getting at."

With that, he looked out again and fixed on a point in the distance.

Anna folded her arms. "What about you? What experience do you have? Have you ever been in a real fight?"

Ben smiled. "I've had the odd altercation in the past."

"I see, because you look like a milk boy."

Ben's tired smile widened. "Rule number one: never underestimate anyone."

"It's just because you're supposed to be the one protecting me. And I don't quite get why."

Ben looked at her. "Did you trust Mo?"

Anna bit her lip at the mention of the name. "Yes. Of course."

Ben nodded. "And he trusted me."

Then his eyes fell on a small shelf lined with books lined up neatly. One caught his eye directly. He walked over and pulled it out. Yes, it was the book *Fool on the Hill*.

"This was a gift from Mo," she said. "He said I should definitely read it."

"Did you?"

Anna screwed up her face. "The story was nice. But I'm more into series."

Ben nodded, then looked out the window. "They're here!"

"What?!" Anna tried to step to the window, but Ben pushed her aside. Then he pointed outside. Cautiously, she looked in the indicated direction.

At first she could see nothing. Then, however, she made out some figures approaching the house and behaving conspicuously inconspicuous. Everything about them just screamed that they did not belong here.

"It's going to look similar out front," Ben observed.

"So where do we go now?"

"To the roof."

Anna looked at him. "To the *roof?* Then that's where we'll be trapped, isn't it? There's nowhere to go from there!"

"Yes, there is. On the other roof."

Anna's eyes grew wide. "You're kidding!"

Ben's eyes were emotionless. "Mo's dead. I'm not joking. You're not going to die."

Anna just nodded and her eyes filled with tears, which she wiped away. "Okay."

"Ready?"

She laughed wanly. "Do I have a choice?"

"No."

She shrugged her shoulders. "Then I'm ready."

Ben nodded. "Good, then let's go."

With that, he pulled out a knife and held it in Anna's direction, who raised her hands dismissively.

"What do you want me to do with this?"

"Use it. Aim for the soft areas of the body. Belly. Neck. Eyes. Genitals."

Anna took it hesitantly and Ben turned, carefully opening the apartment door. Listening for any sound, he entered the hallway. Immediately the motion detector lights came on.

He ran to the stairs and did not turn around. He could hear Anna following close behind him. She might be afraid, but she also wanted to live. He certainly hadn't convinced her completely, but he was her only option. She realized that she was really in danger now, more than ever before.

The stairs ended in a hallway that had several doors and one that officially led outside. Ben headed for it, but Anna held him back.

"It's locked. Wait, I have the key." With that, she took out a small bunch of keys, with five keys hanging from it. After a short search, she found the right one and opened the door.

Once they slipped through, Anna locked the door and looked back at Ben.

"Now what?"

They were on what appeared to be a rooftop terrace of sorts, used by several people. There was a Hollywood swing, various tables and garden chairs. There were also numerous plants that made everything look like a rooftop garden.

If the circumstances were different, it would have been a truly beautiful place where one could simply unwind. Now, however, there was no time for that.

Ben walked to the edge of the roof, which was enclosed by a balustrade, and looked down, then over at the adjacent house.

"You can't be serious now!" Anna stated, instinctively taking a step back. "I thought you were really joking. We'd hide out here somewhere and just make it look like we went over there!"

"We have to get over there. We're trapped here!"

Anna snorted. "Then why did you lead us up here?"

"So we could jump over to the other house."

Anna threw her hands in the air. "Couldn't you have said that before, that you actually meant it? Because then I would have said absolutely not!"

Ben looked at Anna. "Would you rather try your luck with those guys down there?"

She remained silent and chewed her bottom lip. Then she shook her head in annoyance. "Shit!"

As she stepped to the edge and looked down, she felt hot and cold. Three stories were already very high and the other roof seemed very far away.

"I can't do that!"

"Very few people are good at dying. And yet you will if you stay here."

"There must be another way!"

Ben looked toward the door. "Sure. The other way is through about a dozen armed men."

Anna looked angry. "I'm beginning to understand why Mo almost never mentioned you. Your attitude is very depressing."

Ben took a breath. "I'll make you a deal: I'll jump over it and get help. And you stay here and hold them off as long as you can."

Anna's eyes twinkled. "I hate you!"

Ben smiled. "Good, hate can give you incredible powers and make you do things you never thought you could."

She gazed into his eyes, then looked back at the other house. "I know that all too well, I'm afraid. Don't worry. But how do we get over there now? Isn't there some other way? Anything where we don't die right away?"

Ben looked toward the door, then walked to one of the edges and looked over. "Could you do that?"

Anna joined him and looked down at the balcony that was there. "As an alternative to jumping over there? Yes. Hmm. Would have to be the Müllers' balcony."

"Okay. We'll take the balconies then."

"Balcon*ies?* Plural?"

Ben nodded. "First that one, then the one below it."

Anna shook her head. "You really have a sense of humor."

Before Ben could answer, something pounded on the door.

"But I guess I can get used to it," was all Anna said, and began to climb over the balustrade. "Will that door hold?"

"Not for too long. It's designed so no one can break in through it. No one thought of breaking out."

Just then the door burst off its hinges and immediately three men appeared, dressed in black, who could have been spitting images of those who had attacked Mo and Ben in the apartment, as if they all had the same outfitter. And they looked very angry.

Anna cried out and dropped down. Ben risked a quick glance to see if she had made it to the balcony okay, then turned to the men. They were menacingly close and attacked immediately. The largest of them came through the middle and struck at Ben. Ben dodged, blocked the arm, but could not counterattack, because the next one already kicked him, which he had to dodge.

The third, who had not yet attacked him, went to the balustrade and looked over. When he saw Anna, his face contorted and he started to climb down. Ben saw this, grabbed one of the chairs and hurled it at him, causing the man to lose his footing. He spun in the air and slammed his head into the iron balcony railing barely a yard away from Anna. The crack suggested that he had crushed his skull, the crunch that he had broken his neck as well. Anna cried out as he simply lay in front of her like a wet sack of meat, the blood from his cracked skull spreading out in a dark pool.

His hunky partner looked over the balustrade and his face turned angry red. With his eyes distorted with hate, he looked at Ben. The giant reached behind him and took out a long knife. His partner did the same.

Ben reached behind him and pulled out the pistol. Before the two realized it, he had already pulled the trigger repeatedly and put bullets in each of their chests and their foreheads. Both were thrown backwards by the force and also fell over the balustrade. On their way down, they banged on the balcony railing, then continued to plummet downward, coming to rest at the bottom with a sickening sound.

Anna was shaking all over. In a very short time, she had witnessed how three men had died brutally before her eyes. In front of her and below on the lawn lay various bodies, which in their grotesque contortions barely resembled people.

When she looked up, she saw Ben looking down over the balustrade. Before she could say anything, a noise sounded from the roof and Ben had disappeared.

Ben turned around and saw more men coming out of the door. Immediately he fired more shots, all of which hit their target. But then his magazine was empty. Without hesitation, he threw the pistol at the next man who came through the door, so that it hit him squarely in the nose. As Ben lunged toward him, he grabbed the large knife the giant had dropped and struck his attacker's arm with it. The force of the blow and the sharpness of the knife, which was more like a machete, were enough to sever his arm cleanly.

Screaming, the man went to his knees while blood spurted from the stump of his arm. Ben paid no more attention to him and lunged at the next man, kicking him in the chest, only to immediately lash out with the knife at another attacker, cutting him horizontally across the face. When the victim swayed to the side, Ben turned and struck with the knife at the man he had just kicked and was now getting up again. The cut went right through his throat and made him sink to the ground, gasping.

Ben grabbed the man's gun and immediately fired at the door. A man ran into the middle of the hail of bullets and was pulled backwards. Ben stopped firing, changed the magazine and waited. When someone appeared, Ben fired immediately, then waited again.

Continuing to aim at the door with one hand, he checked the bodies for more magazines, which he pocketed. Then he moved slowly to the balustrade, only to jump down.

Anna cried out. "What the fuck is going on?!"

Without answering her question, Ben pushed her aside and aimed upward. When a head appeared, he fired immediately. Blood and brains splashed down like rain while the rest disappeared from sight again.

Anna screamed again as she tried in vain to get rid of the splashes of blood and brains that had hit her face. Ben, on the other hand, shot at the glass of the balcony door, then reached in and opened the door. Quickly pulling Anna with him, he crossed the room with her and pushed her behind the wall of the next door while aiming outside.

A foot appeared and Ben fired. At that, the man to whom the foot belonged fell down screaming and slammed on the balcony.

Now it was not only Anna who screamed, an elderly couple also looked frightened from their bedroom into the hallway.

"Hide!" shouted Ben, and the couple panicked and did as he said.

As Ben continued to aim for the balcony door, he slowly moved to the front door and undid the locks there. The key was in it and he slowly turned it around.

"Do you have a car?" asked Ben quietly.

"Yes," Anna breathed. "I always park on the other side."

Ben nodded, then opened the door almost silently. As soon as he stepped out, the lights came on. To Anna's amazement, however, he walked back inside and pulled her to the side into the corner behind the door, which he left open.

The next moment Anna heard voices coming from the staircase as well as from the balcony. When she could make out figures, she had to suppress a scream. The figures, however, ran past her and Ben into the stairwell, where they met more and apparently moved downstairs.

When nothing more could be heard, Ben slipped out from behind the door and closed it carefully, then went back to the balcony, his gun cocked.

The man he had shot in the foot still lay there, left behind by his comrades. Completely surprised, he wanted to scream. Ben kicked him in the head, which crashed against the wall behind him with full force and with a sickening sound, leaving a dark red stain.

"Oh, my God!" whispered Anna. "You're crazy! You're sick!"

Ben didn't care. He looked over the balcony. "Can you jump down there?"

Anna's eyes grew wide. "Damn, that's too far!"

Ben pointed to the tree, a birch, that stood between the parallel balconies. "Then we'll take that one."

"It doesn't look very sturdy, though," Anna pointed out.

"Jump it, then."

"Screw you!" Anna hissed, making her way to the tree. Uncertainly, she looked down, but then climbed over the railing, took a breath and jumped into the tree.

The next moment the apartment door was kicked open and a broad-shouldered man came stumbling in, followed by someone rather slighter in contrast to him. Ben jumped to the side to get a better shot and fired. He hit the weaker of the two, first only in the arm, but then in the chest and head, but could not prevent the other from jumping at him, so that Ben's pistol flew down over the railing.

While Anna desperately held on to the tree and slowly moved down, the two men wrestled with each other. The broad Russian relied on his brute strength alone, while Ben moved into hand-to-hand combat, taking a few hard hits at first. Then, however, he managed to block the Russian's attacks and to strike at him in turn, while deflecting all the attacks. Again and again he punched the attacker in the face with his fists and elbows, turning him into an increasingly bloody mass.

The man staggered backwards against the railing like a battered boxer on the ropes. Quickly Ben took a running start and jumped at the man to tumble over the railing with him. In the process, Ben yanked him around so that it was the man who crashed hard to the floor while Ben landed on top of him.

The Russian groaned and spat blood. As he tried to turn to the side, Ben crouched on top of him and continued to beat him until he stopped moving. Breathing heavily, he looked down at the man for another moment. Then he finally rose, went to his pistol and picked it up.

When Anna reached the ground, Ben gave her no respite. He pushed her against the wall and waited. As soon as more men showed themselves, he shot each one directly in the head. The shots were barely audible through the silencer, while the sound of the head bursting open sounded incredibly loud in Anna's ears, reminding her of a watermelon falling on a hard floor.

Instead of screaming, Anna just closed her eyes and opened them only when she felt a tug on her right wrist.

Ben directed them to the trees that offered them shelter. Before they went any further, he oriented himself to see if any more men would appear while he refilled his pistol with a new magazine.

"Where's your car?"

Anna gulped. "Over there – on the other side."

Ben took a breath and nodded.

Cautiously, as if they were being hunted by a dangerous predator, they slowly ventured forward, taking advantage of every shadow and cover they could find.

"We have to go over there through the playground," Anna said.

Ben didn't like that at all. The trees gave them a good hiding place, but they had to cross open ground to get to the playground, and the playground equipment hardly offered any protection. Nevertheless, they had to leave as soon as possible.

Looking around, they finally just walked across without anyone noticing them. As they approached the parking lot, Anna pulled out her car keys, pressed the button, and immediately the lights on her Golf came on.

In the next instant, the attack occurred.

Before the bullet could hit her, Ben pushed Anna aside, then dodged it himself. In doing so, he stumbled at first, but then quickly regained his footing and fired. Again and again.

Anna was grabbed by the hair and pulled up. But then her instinct took over. In the next moment, she grabbed her attacker's arm and spun him around, causing him to let go and kicked him, as she had learned to do. She hit him in the knee and heard a cry of pain, whereupon she punched him in the face. Still, the man grabbed at her, clasping her left hand with a grip as strong as a vice.

Anna reached for the knife Ben had given her. Without thinking, she stabbed the man until the blade penetrated to the shaft next to his neck. The man's grip loosened and he sank to the grass with his last breath.

Before Anna even realized what she had done, the next man came. As he approached her, he pulled out a knife himself and Anna thought her heart would stop. Before he reached her, however, he was suddenly yanked backwards as a bullet slammed into his chest.

Startled, she backed away, turning around to see a man come very close to Ben and point his gun at his head, as if he were simply going to execute him. Anna cried out, but Ben had long since reacted. He dodged to the side, punched the attacker in the arm, then pulled his legs away and slammed them onto the hood of the car. He turned the attacker's pistol against himself and pulled the trigger. Once. Twice. Three times.

Inhaling deeply through his nose, Ben straightened up and looked around. Then he wrestled the pistol from the dead man and picked up his own.

"To the car!" he said curtly, and Anna followed him as if in a trance. She picked up the keys she had dropped and handed them to him. While she sat down in the passenger seat, mechanically fastening the seat belt, he was already starting the car, reversing and then just driving off.

"Who the hell are you?!" shouted Anna, looking around to see if any of the attackers were still pursuing her, but nothing was moving anywhere.

Ben took a breath. "Someone who wants to fulfill a friend's last wish."

"But you're not just a banker, geez!" Anna was still beside herself. "I mean, I know Mo trained in self-protection for years and his father was a cop, but *that?* You don't learn that in a class! You killed those guys without batting an eye. And how come you're such a good shot? And fighter? Who are you? Where did you learn all that?"

Ben was silent. Anna's words had triggered a flood of images and emotions in him that he didn't need right now. He had to concentrate, because it certainly wasn't over yet.

Already he saw in the rearview mirror that a car had turned onto the road some distance behind them and accelerated.

"Could you say something, please?"

Ben looked in the rearview mirror again. "I just want to make sure no one is following us."

Anna laughed mirthlessly. "Who? You've killed everyone, haven't you? Everyone who attacked us is dead!"

"I was just protecting you."

As he continued to look in the rearview mirror, she looked around in horror. She clearly saw the headlights of the other car, which she couldn't quite make out.

"That could be anyone," she said.

"I'd rather not assume that."

The car followed them, but then turned off. Ben nodded, but remained alert.

Anna swallowed and looked ahead again. "What are you going to do now? Do you have a plan?"

Ben nodded. "Mo was right. We have to stop them. Until we stop them, you won't be safe. We really need to know what's on the list. In addition, we need to know what's on the computer."

"But surely they'll be guarding that?"

"Nevertheless, this is our only chance. And we have to get there fast, before they delete everything."

Anna shook her head. "You're leading us into the lion's den with this, aren't you?"

"Call me Ben."

Anna took a deep breath. "Ben." She looked out the window, and nodded. "Anna."

Ben nodded curtly as well. "Yes, Anna. You're right about us heading straight into the lion's den."

Anna seemed to resign and shook her head. "First you save me so I can escape them, and now you want to drive me into their arms for better or worse."

"I'd rather know you're in a safe place, but the danger is too great that I need you to get the information. Besides, it's the only way I can keep an eye on you. Unfortunately, though, you can't have one without the other."

Anna exhaled. "I believe you, unfortunately. Otherwise I would have left long ago." She was silent for a moment and then looked at Ben. "Where should we go first now?"

"For now, we'll find a safe hiding place. There we'll decipher the coded list."

"You can do that?"

"Yes. The code is based on Mo and my favorite book. When we wanted to send each other co-designated messages, we've always used that book, or rather a specific page."

Anna nodded. "If you don't know that and you don't know the page, you're screwed. So the list wouldn't have done these guys any good."

"No, not without the book and knowing which page to use and how."

Anna took a breath and shook her head with a resigned smile. Then she looked at Ben. "I'm sorry about your friend. Mo was really..."

Ben nodded, but there was a flash in his eyes. "Yeah."

"And he told you to look out for me?"

Ben nodded. "Yes. It was the last thing he wanted."

Anna shook her head. "Unbelievable. Why did he do that? I mean, he was dying and he was still thinking about me?"

"That's how Mo was, that's how I met him. I don't mean exactly like that. In the beginning he was very distant and would have preferred to get rid of me. Later I found out that he was the Mo I really got to know. He was always worried about others. He preferred that something happened to him rather than someone else. Family and friends came first for him. Equal. He himself, well he himself didn't play a big role for himself."

"But to you."

Ben took a breath. "Mo and his father were the most important people to me."

Anna nodded. "It sounds like you won't let those responsible for his death get away with it."

Ben took a breath and he gripped the steering wheel tightly until his knuckles stood out white.

They were silent for the rest of the drive. Anna glanced out the window, trying to get some sort of orientation as to where Ben was taking her, but couldn't make out anything. When he drove into a wooded area, she began to worry, but said nothing. Finally, Ben stopped and turned off the engine.

Anna watched Ben, who continued to look ahead. Then he looked in the rearview mirror, waited, and got out. Anna followed him, but looked around in irritation.

"You don't really want to go into the woods now, do you? It's totally dark."

Ben nodded. "If anyone followed us, they'll be in trouble there."

Anna became cynical. "So will we. You can't see your hand in front of your face."

"I know my way around here. Mo and I spent a lot of time here in our youth."

"Yes. With flashlights, or during the day."

Ben smiled. "I showed him how to lose pursuers here. This is more useful than always facing a fight."

Anna shook her head and followed Ben. "What about those guys just now?"

"There was no way to lose them then."

Ben waited until Anna was close to him. "Always walk right behind me. Then nothing will happen to you."

"Great. That makes me feel a lot better."

Ben was virtually creeping like a cat into the completely dark forest, while Anna felt like a big elephant as she kept stepping on branches and barely avoiding tripping.

"Who the hell are you? I mean, you don't learn something like that while camping, do you? What special unit did you used to belong to? No... you're too young for that. Aren't you? And when did you do your banking apprenticeship then?"

"Boy Scouts!" Ben suggested.

Anna expelled an annoyed breath. "Yeah, sure. That's the kind of thing you learn all about in the Boy Scouts!"

"We'd better be quiet. Just because we don't see our pursuers doesn't mean we're not being followed."

Anna shook her head. "And you really advise people on money investments? With your positive attitude, I find that hard to believe. And if we don't find a place to hide soon, our pursuers won't have to worry about me anymore, because I'm sure to break my neck."

"We're here," Ben stated, and Anna looked around in irritation.

"Now what makes this place better than all the others we've passed?"

Ben smiled. "Scouts' secret!"

With that, he squatted down and pulled out the list. Anna turned on the light on her cell phone and set it to the dimmest setting to stay behind Ben and shine from there. She herself could hardly make out anything, but Ben seemed to have less trouble.

He looked at the piece of paper and the completely random looking sequences of letters and numbers.

"Do you have a pen?" he finally asked.

She rummaged in her backpack and handed him a black pen. Again Ben seemed to think, then began to write, lining up letter after letter, adding numbers, until finally he had translated the entire list.

Anna looked more closely. "What's this? Names?"

Ben nodded. "Not real names, but code names."

"Isegrim, Adebar, Reineke, Braun, Hylax," Anna read aloud. "These are names of animals in the fable."

Ben nodded. "And the one behind that seems to be account numbers. And then numbers... each a date, I would say. And then initials."

Anna nodded. "Yeah, looks like it. But what does that mean?"

Ben was silent for a moment. "I don't know. They just seem to be short notes."

Anna's eyes narrowed. "And what does it say down there?"

Anna pointed to a line Ben hadn't translated.

"That appears to be the path for getting to the data on the computer."

Anna nodded. "Was that all Mo gave you?"

"No. He still gave me his cell phone. I guess there's more evidence there."

Anna looked at Ben. "And where is this cell phone?"

"Hidden. With a note so it will be given to someone I trust."

"Police? I thought you said you didn't trust the police."

Ben's expression grew more serious. "No. Worse."

Anna nodded. Suddenly she startled. "What is it?"

Ben came up and looked around. That's when he felt a twinge in his throat and his whole perception became blurred from one moment to the next.

The last thing he saw was Anna's face leaning over him and then looking to the side.

"Shit!" she hissed.

Then everything was black.

8

The cell phone rang. When it did, it was never good news. If it did so on a night when Frank Wolters was not on duty, something had gone very badly wrong.

Without turning on the light, he answered the call. "Yes?"

Whoever had called him had not done so by mistake, and certainly no one had dialed the wrong number.

"Strobel here."

Wolters knew Strobel. She was one of the data analysts and one of the few he trusted. She had been grateful to him for standing up for her, even though she seemed so nervous that she seemed unfit for the job. Because of his support, she was allowed to stay and prove herself. Now she was one of the top analysts whose opinion often decided danger ratings.

Strobel was a night person. Wolters was not surprised that she was still working at this hour. That she called him, however, was disconcerting enough.

"I apologize for disturbing you so late at this hour," she said, but Wolters brushed that right aside.

"Strobel, please, you will never have to apologize to me for doing your job. What's it all about? I hope some assholes didn't set fire to another asylum home."

"No. It's about Mohamed Aslan. He was murdered."

If Wolters had not been fully awake until just now, all fatigue disappeared instantly, something he had felt more and more often since he had passed fifty.

"How?"

"According to the police, it was a robbery. His body has both stab and gunshot wounds."

"Crap!"

"Any leads on a possible perpetrator?"

"The report just came in. When I saw the name, I decided to let you know right away."

Strobel had proven to be as loyal as Wolters suspected. He gave her time to sift through the other information.

"There are further reports of dead, Russians found near the scene of the crime. In addition, reports of strange occurrences are piling up. Gunshots. Chases. Fights and more deaths. At 38 Sonnenallee."

Wolters closed his eyes. *So it had happened.*

He took a breath and stood up. He would not get any more sleep that night, because he had to leave very quickly.

"Send everything to my cell phone. I'll get a picture on the spot."

"All right. Shall I inform the incident commander there?"

Wolters snorted. "You mean the one we're already monitoring because of his connection to the right-wing scene? No. I'll possibly inform him on the spot."

"All right. Do you need a strike team?"

Wolters was silent for a moment. "Yes. But if it's as I suspect, we need something else entirely."

"Like what?"

"Body bags. Lots and lots of body bags."

9

Everyone knew how Gunther had really died. Fenrir may have killed him, but it was Finn who had led him into the trap. That it was actually Gunther who had waylaid Finn to feast on Finn being mauled by the black beast didn't matter.

Finn had told no one what had happened, nor would anyone have cared. Everyone had thought it for sure, but it didn't matter.

Finn had stayed underwater for a long time, just drifting until he truly couldn't manage to hold his breath. When he finally dared, he only saw from a distance how Fenrir was still feasting on Gunther's corpse, probably because he was enraged that his usual prey had escaped him.

When Finn returned, there was no cheering. Too many promising youngsters had not returned. And he, of all people, from whom little or nothing was expected, had survived. No one would voice their disapproval of that, but Finn could see it in their eyes.

Later he learned that Erik and Matt had been there and really saw what had happened between him and Gunther. And what had happened afterwards. None of them mourned Gunther a tear, but even they knew that the real way would have been for Gunther to become a warrior and not him, Finn, the outsider.

Odin saw this differently. He put his huge paw on Finn's shoulder from one hand and looked at him with those dark eyes that made one thing clear to Finn and, really, to anyone: Fenrir was not the most dangerous creature in the community, for Odin did not command the black beast without reason. "Well done, Finn. I am very proud of you."

These words, audible to all, were more than anyone could have expected. And yet, Finn's fear went through him. He had always managed to stay out of the eyes of the elders and not stand out so much. He did what he was told, but didn't stand out.

But then the fight with Gunther had come, in which he had been chosen as the loser. But he won and destroyed the former exemplary youth forever by smashing his knee and hand with a simple stone. He could also have split his skull, but something held Finn back then. If Gunther had been in his place, he would not have hesitated a second, Finn was sure. But he was not Gunther. And he wasn't one of the others either. He just wanted to survive until... Yes, until when exactly?

After he had finally defeated Gunther, it was no more necessary to lay him low or hold back. Now he had the full attention of the ancients, and especially Odin.

One day the leader of their community came to him and gave him a little puppy. In contrast to the other offspring of the wolf-like fighting dogs, this one was downright puny and looked sickly.

"Here. This is for you," Odin had said as he handed Finn the puppy. "Actually, he would have served only as food, but I saw something in his eyes that I saw in yours. A fire that no one seemed to notice. I think you could underestimate the little guy, just like you were underestimated. That's why you'll do well together. I want you to prove that I'm right. Take care of him, raise him, and make him as good a comrade as you are."

To be given a mission by Odin meant to fulfill it. There was no failure. His word was more important than any other. But of all the assignments, it was this one that Finn was very happy to accept.

He looked at the puppy and the puppy looked at him. When the little dog licked his hand, he knew they would be friends forever.

Why he named him Ben, Finn could not say even years later. He never talked about it, and yet everyone seemed to know that he had not given his dog an expected name, such an inappropriate one. But Odin seemed to tolerate it and so nobody said anything.

Ben grew into a handsome wolfhound who lived up to everything that was expected of the dogs of the community. His body under his shimmering bluish fur was muscular, his build strong, and he was almost the tallest of all the dogs, apart from Fenrir, of course. In the hunts, there was no team that harmonized as perfectly as Finn and Ben. Therefore, no one was allowed to interfere in the upbringing, which some people found fault with. But since that fateful day Finn was under Odin's protection and so was Ben.

Ben was Finn's best friend. And his only true one. Fate had connected them in a way Finn could not find the words for. But without him, Finn would not have known where he was now.

As Finn stood in front of Odin with Ben beside him, the entire community were around them. All eyes rested on them and Finn sensed something was about to happen. Something bad. It couldn't be any other way.

Odin sat on his big wooden chair, decorated with all kinds of symbols, runes and carvings, which is why *everyone just called it the throne. Next to him sat Fenrir, attentively as ever, watching Ben, while Odin's eyes rested on Finn's alone. Finn dared not resist that gaze.*

"To lead is to show strength. Determination," Odin explained, and Finn wasn't sure if the words applied to everyone, as they always did, or not to him alone.

"What's the most important thing?" asked Odin, and Finn wasn't the only one who immediately shouted out loud: "No retreating! No giving up! No mercy!"

Odin showed no emotion. "And this is achieved through action. Directly. No thinking about it. Knowledge. The community depends on each individual living by it, not just the leaders. Obeying leads to strength. Action leads to strength. No retreating! No surrender! No mercy! Everyone must obey, or we will perish in the world out there!"

Finn continued to hold Odin's gaze and Odin smiled.

"You have exceeded all of our expectations, Finn. You have become an exemplary member of our community and have become the focus of everyone's attention, especially mine. You have also exceeded my expectations as far as your companion is concerned. When I gave him to you and told you to take care of him, he was small, puny, and nothing indicated that he would one day become the animal we now see before us. In many tests, you have proven how strong your bond is. Impressive. Most impressive. Exemplified by him, you have proven that we can still expect great things from you."

Odin paused, and Finn felt a chill run down his spine. When the leader of the community spoke, his voice was perfectly calm and his gaze emotionless as before.

"Take your knife and cut his body open. Look into his eyes as he dies."

No one dared to say anything. There was no murmur. Finn knew that some were surely smiling inside, but no one would show it.

All eyes rested on Finn and saw that he had not drawn his knife directly. Instead, he stood there and didn't move, continuing to look into Odin's eyes. He didn't let on, but everyone could see in his eyes what was going on inside him. Finn had not carried out his order. He had not drawn his knife and thrust it into the body of his dog. That was treason.

As emotionless as before, Odin spoke only one word. "Sic."

Immediately Fenrir leaped forward and stopped directly at Finn. Already he saw the black terror leaping toward his throat. But before the hellhound could reach Finn, he was yanked aside in a leap.

Without hesitation, Ben threw himself at Fenrir and both went down in a wild tangle. Ben had managed to grab Fenrir by the neck so that the huge animal could not snap at him. On the contrary, for the first time a conspecific had him by the throat and wrestled him to the ground and onto his back. A humiliation.

Blood oozed from the wound Ben had inflicted on him, but the pain only made Fenrir fiercer. As tight as Ben had grabbed him, it wasn't tight enough.

With all his might, Fenrir tore free and Ben could no longer hold him. Immediately he followed up, but now Fenrir was prepared. Ben had brought him to the brink of defeat and now he would make him pay. Fenrir had no more eyes for Finn. If his master had given him an order to let go of Ben and pounce on Finn, he would have done it without hesitation, but the order failed to materialize.

The two dogs, whose ancestry went back to the first great wolves that once hunted together with the first humans, circled each other. Incessantly they bared their teeth, leaving no doubt that only one would leave this place alive.

And then they collided and Finn's heart stopped. Again and again the mouths snapped at each other. They inflicted wounds on each other that spurted blood. Ben seemed truly equal to Fenrir. But Fenrir was not the most feared of all for nothing. And just when Finn dared to hope that Ben might have a chance... Fenrir grabbed Ben by the neck and hurled him to the ground with one mighty movement. In the next moment his teeth buried themselves in Ben's abdomen and tore it open brutally.

Ben yelped. Finn had never heard such a heart-rending sound and it truly made him tremble. Ben literally slumped down and now all the terror that a sentient being was capable of was mixed into his wailing sound.

Fenrir crept around Ben, circled him and gloated over the suffering of the one who had dared to grab him by the throat and throw him on his back. Under the watchful eyes of his master and everyone, he feasted on the terror and suffering he had caused.

He stood in front of Ben as if he wanted him to see that he would now make him suffer even more. But as he was about to lunge at Ben for the final death blow, he was rammed again, this time by Finn. Finn stabbed Fenrir with the knife as they rolled across the floor. Finn's knife slipped and in the very next moment Fenrir's head wheeled around and grabbed Finn's arm. A sharp pain chased up Finn's shoulder and he dropped the knife, but managed to free his arm.

Fenrir hesitated only a moment and went right back into the attack, leaping at Finn. But Finn was prepared, didn't care about his wound and jumped towards Fenrir. Before he could grab again, Finn grabbed him and flung him to the ground like a wrestler. Fenrir tried to get back to his feet immediately, but Finn grabbed him, wrapped his arms around Fenrir's body and held him tightly against him.

Fenrir growled and snapped, but could not wrestle Finn away. Finn squeezed even tighter, increasing Fenrir's rage into frenzy. Finn did not let up. Instead, he only gripped Fenrir's body tighter. Fenrir's growls turned into yelps.

More and more desperate became the terrible beast, now presenting a picture of misery. Nevertheless, Fenrir did not give up and moved more and more violently. And when it already looked like Fenrir could break away and his yelp turned into a growl again, Finn let himself fall backwards and lifted Fenrir above him.

When Fenrir's back hit the hard ground, everyone could hear the cracking sound. In the next moment, the yelp and whine was even more pathetic than Ben's.

Powerless, Finn stood up and staggered to his knife. With trembling hands he clasped the handle and stood over Fenrir, whose front legs were desperately trying to lift the body, but the rear part no longer obeyed him. Without paying any further attention to Fenrir, Finn staggered over to Ben and sank to the ground beside his friend. Tenderly he stroked Ben's head. Ben whimpered, but still licked Finn's hand.

Finn lowered his head and pressed his forehead to Ben's. Then he stabbed and rammed Ben's head into the ground. He stabbed and rammed the knife into his friend's heart. The whimpering stopped.

As sudden rain fell on the two, Finn remained in posture while no sound was heard around him. All were silent. Then he heard footsteps approaching through the rain. Finn didn't have to look up to know who it was.

Odin passed Fenrir, still whimpering in the mud, desperately trying to get up as if that alone would end his suffering. In vain. His former master did not dignify him with a glance and would not release him from his suffering as Finn had done with his friend. He had lost and disgraced his master.

When Odin stopped in front of Finn, Finn raised his head and looked the leader of the community almost defiantly in the face. No movement showed itself there. Then Odin suddenly struck and his powerful fist hit Finn in the temple.

Unconscious, Finn went down next to his dead friend, while Odin stood over him, looking down at him. He simply turned and walked out of the square past everyone who silently followed him with their gazes. As Odin passed the dogs, he let out only one command.

"Eat."

Drooling, the dogs dashed off and pounced on the still-living Fenrir, whose yelps grew ever quieter. Finn and Ben, however, did not touch them, as if they knew the command did not include them.

10

"Ah, he's coming round!"

Ben heard the voice as if from far away, but felt the blow with the flat of his hand.

"Come on, now! Wake up!"

Another blow with the flat of his hand. This time harder.

Ben concentrated on the pain, trying to perceive it in its entirety, trying to pull himself out of his unconsciousness.

Laughter.

"You got hit pretty good!"

Another blow. Again, harder than before. Or was he coming more and more to consciousness and could feel everything better now?

Ben listened inside himself. His legs still felt numb, his hands too. He felt they were tied up. His head felt as if it were wrapped in cotton. This feeling gradually disappeared.

He was still in the forest. Tied up and leaning against a tree. Opening his eyes a little, he saw several lights, flashlights. Directly in front of him squatted a man with a rather unfriendly expression on his face. In the corner of his mouth he had a toothpick, which he kept pushing from side to side. Judging by his accent, he was clearly of Russian origin.

Again, Ben was struck by a blow that finally brought him back to the here and now. Nevertheless, he kept his eyes closed and his head hanging. The darkness would also allow him to examine his bonds without anyone noticing.

Ben heard another voice. "Alexei, someone's coming!" The man in front of him stood up, presumably Alexei.

"Pretty busy here tonight," he said with amusement.

"Who do we have here? Guys, you're meeting a celebrity now!"

Ben opened his eyes a crack, but without changing the position of his head. The area was well lit by the large flashlights and he could make out four men who seemed to belong together. They were joined by another man who was not Russian.

"Matteo. What brings you to this deserted area? And at this time of night, too?"

Matteo laughed, spread his arms and embraced Alexei, kissing him right and left on the cheek, while the other three Russians did not take their eyes off him.

"Ciao, Alexei. I guess I'm here for the same reason you guys are. My boss has also become a bit nervous about the events of this night. He has questions he's only too happy to have answered."

"If you're looking for this Anna Kerkov, she's not here anymore. Our boss also has questions and called her in."

Ben had trouble sitting still. He would have liked to jump up and punch Alexei to tell him where Anna was.

Matteo nodded and put his hands over each other in front of him.

"So to the old sugar factory. Are you still using it?"

Alexei raised his finger to his lips. "Trade secret. But since you've already figured it out yourself, yes. I can understand Russev there. It's secluded there, and you're on your own."

Matteo nodded. "Yes, I once had the dubious honor."

Alexei raised his hands. "Wasn't anything personal. After all, I've fallen into your clutches before. Business is business, and sometimes you get in each other's way."

Matteo smiled mirthlessly. "Yes. Do you think Russev will mind if I sit in on the conversation so I can report back to my boss?"

Alexei laughed. "I think your presence might make Russev a little nervous. Besides, he's probably still in a bad mood with you. That business in Berlin is still bothering him."

Matteo raised his hands defensively. "I had nothing to do with that!"

"But it had your handwriting on it."

"Hey, we don't get in each other's way. That's the deal."

Alexei let a few moments pass, then nodded. "Yeah. Russev doesn't really believe you guys will stick to the deal anymore, though. And now we have the mess. And I'm here to clean it all up."

Matteo nodded. "Isn't that usually Sergey's job?"

Alexei laughed derisively. "Ah, were you expecting him here? Fancy another dance? Didn't turn out so well for you last time. Well, anyway. Sergey screwed up and now I have to straighten it out. This Anna is with Russev now and this other guy too. That will take the problems off the table tonight and then it was all just a nuisance."

Matteo nodded and then pointed in Ben's direction. "And who's that guy?"

Alexei shrugged. "A nobody. He just happened to be with that Anna girl. Must be a friend of that fucking

Turk we whacked. I don't know. We should just take this Anna to Russev and keep an eye on that one until we can get him to Russev too."

Matteo walked up to Ben and squatted in front of him, looking him over closely.

"A nobody, huh? I saw what that nobody did."

Matteo stood up again and Alexei spread his arms, laughing. "What do you want me to say? I have no idea who that guy is. His friend was snooping around and Sergey didn't finish him off properly. Even got some himself. And now we're here. A big mess, yes. But it will all work out. And then everything will be like before."

Matteo nodded. "Well, not quite."

Alexei was irritated, but laughed and looked to his men, who were also laughing. "Don't worry, Matteo. We'll get this fixed."

Matteo smiled and nodded. The next moment he pulled out a pistol with a silencer. Before the four Russians could do anything, four soft shots rang out and Ben heard four bodies fall to the ground. Matteo waited a moment, then slowly walked to the bodies and shot each one again in the head.

Ben did not move, but he clearly heard Matteo come to him and crouch in front of him again. When Ben didn't move, Matteo pressed the still-hot end of the silencer onto a free spot on his shoulder blade.

Ben cried out and Matteo pressed a little harder before pulling the gun back again.

"So our sleepyhead is awake," Matteo noted, rising. "I guess you've been awake for quite a while now."

Ben breathed heavily, fighting the pain. He looked with piercing eyes toward Matteo, who shone a flashlight into his face.

"What's your name?" Matteo demanded.

Ben hesitated for a moment and took a few deep breaths, his cheek muscles playing and revealing his anger all too clearly. "Ben," he finally managed.

Matteo nodded. "All right, Ben. Who are you? I know all the players in this strange scenario, but you're a blank slate. Truly no one had you on their radar, and yet here you are. Why?" He paused for a moment before continuing, as if not really expecting an answer. "Oh yeah, your friend was murdered, all right. He stuck his nose into things that weren't his business. Couldn't keep his hands off it. Couldn't let it go. And unfortunately started a chain reaction that led us here, and unfortunately it doesn't end here. No, I regret. Good Alexei was completely wrong when he believed that everything would be all right again. Even before that, the old order had begun to shake. I would never have believed that it would happen like this and right now. It was clear that something would happen, but not yet."

Matteo squatted in front of Ben again and looked directly at him. "Your friend made quite a mess of everything. Maybe it could have ended with his death, but I don't believe in that either. Well, it doesn't matter now. What does matter, though, because I'm dying to know, is: who are you?

"Your path is paved with a little too many corpses to be ignored. I certainly don't, because that piques my interest directly. What you did there, that was not luck. I admit I don't think much of Russev's men. After all, they are all military trained. Okay, even that doesn't mean much now, but they're certainly ruthless. And yet you've made it this far. So who are you? And what do you know?"

Ben said nothing, just stared at his counterpart with a hateful look.

Matteo just smiled. "You see. That's what I mean. That's not the reaction of someone who doesn't know how to handle a situation like this. You're acting more like a soldier on a mission from which he can't be dissuaded under any circumstances. If I hadn't taken care of these guys, I'm sure you would have."

He waited a moment. Ben remained silent.

"Still nothing to say? Okay, I don't have forever either. You've heard that Anna is with Russev, and I assume he's very displeased about what happened that night. This could be very unpleasant for her, and important questions will be clarified there as well. Therefore, I can't deal with you forever and wait for answers."

Matteo narrowed his eyes. "I'm guessing military. But German? Bund? That would be very strange. Anyway."

With that, he put away his pistol and took out a switchblade instead.

Matteo rolled his eyes and smiled sheepishly. "Yes, I know: what a cliché. An Italian with a switchblade. Let's just say I'm aware of the irony and that's why I have it. Or for nostalgic reasons. Take your pick or leave it. It doesn't matter."

With that, he cut Ben's shirt, but without hurting him.

"Military guys like you always have some kind of tattoo, after all, which might put me on the trail of..."

He paused and shone his light on the large symbol emblazoned on the left side of Ben's chest. For a few moments he couldn't believe what he saw there.

11

"So, you wanted to leave our community?"

Rarely was anger heard in Odin's voice. This was reserved for all the traitors he always spoke of. Finn was now one of them.

He had been tied to a table, his arms and legs bound, as well as his naked torso, so that he could not move.

Only a few were gathered in the hut. Besides Odin and some of the oldest still comrades from Finn's group, Erik, Matt, Gunnar and the others who were to witness Finn's punishment.

"You even dared to endanger the community by letting one of them escape!"

"He was innocent!" spat Finn at Odin.

Odin's face turned angry red. "He was inferior and a danger to everyone. It was only thanks to Erik's prudent intervention that the worst was prevented. He had no qualms about doing the right thing and protecting his community. For this he was also granted the honor of the sign."

With that, Odin stood in front of Erik, who looked at him proudly and presented his left forearm, on the inside of which, just below the elbow, was tattooed a skull, its bone encrusted with all sorts of fine runes. This sign showed the initiates that he had killed for the community and now belonged to the Deathbringers. Henceforth he would bring death to those on behalf of Odin.

"This mark is one of the greatest honors we have to bestow. The bearers are the most honored members of our community."

He turned back to Finn and grabbed his left arm, emblazoned with the same symbol.

"You, too, once earned the honor when you were less restrained. But what you did today was against everything we and this symbol stand for." He let go of Finn's arm and his expression calmed again.

"For that, you will get a new mark. The mark of the outcast, so that everyone of those you tried to save will immediately know who and what you are. Who you consider your equals. Who you prefer to your people, to your comrades, to your blood.

"How dare you! To choose this filth over us! Who, with one look at the symbol, will make you feel their hatred. Who will punish you with contempt. Persecute you. Ostracize you. Spit on. Beat you. Abuse you. And kill you. Because they see you for the scum you are.

"Once we mark you, there will be no place for you to flee to. No one will give you shelter. No one will protect you. You will be ostracized as soon as you see the mark, the symbol.

"Let's see how long you will protect these creatures then, and not resist them when it is you whose skin they claim."

Odin stepped back from the table and the draftsman approached. In his hand he held the tattoo needle with which he had already drawn so many and with which he applied the symbol of hatred over a large area on the left side of Finn's chest while he screamed at the top of his lungs.

12

"Now that's surprising!" Matteo laughed, still trying to classify what he had seen. Then he shook his head. "If those guys had seen that, oh man, they would have made you bleed for it. They would have cut it right out of you.

"And Russev first of all..." he paused. "But your friend is of Turkish descent. How could he be your friend?"

Matteo laughed. "Man, you're puzzling me more and more. Now I want answers more than ever. Who are you? And how did you get involved in all this?"

Ben leaned forward. "I'm a nobody."

Matteo nodded with a laugh. "If you see the symbol, definitely. You'll get killed for that in the circles you've gotten into. It's almost a duty."

He shook his head again. "You little perverted asshole. It will be my pleasure to kill you. Yes, even a fucking duty. So I won't find out who you are from you. That's fine. All that matters now is Anna."

Ben laughed.

Matteo laughed along at first, but then got angry. "What's so damn funny?"

Ben continued to laugh and then seemed to calm down. "It's so funny because it doesn't matter who I am, what the symbol is supposed to be, or what's going on with Anna. Not at this moment."

Matteo clearly showed that he was angry. "So? Then what's important?"

Ben's fist crashed into Matteo's face. "That I'm long past being tied up!"

Ben stood up and Matteo reached into his jacket for his gun. But already Ben was on him, kicking right at the spot. Matteo cried out and pulled out his hand, which contained a pistol, but Ben deflected the bullet with a blow against the barrel. The next moment he applied a lever and Matteo dropped the pistol in pain, but was able to block Ben's next blow and deliver a blow himself that crashed against Ben's forehead, causing him to stagger.

Matteo laughed. "That's good! Just picking you off would have been too easy, too. Too good for you, you Nazi pig!"

With that, he reached behind him and pulled out a hunting knife with a sharp edge on one side and a serrated one on the other.

Ben nodded appreciatively. "Now that's a *real* knife!"

Matteo smiled. "I'm going to enjoy ramming that blade into your eyes! And then I'll cut that damn swastika off your body alive!"

Ben snorted. "The idea isn't as new as you might think!"

Matteo attacked. Ben immediately noticed that Matteo had some experience fighting with a knife. He was not just a street fighter who had learned his skills in the gutters of Palermo. Maybe he had started there, but what he showed revealed a more specialized training.

Ben dodged Matteo's thrust, but he noticed that his senses were not yet reacting as he was used to. Still, he could rely on his trained reactions, which still made him one of the best fighters. Mo had never had a chance against him, just like his father. But there it was never a matter of life and death. This was different here. Matteo not only wanted to hurt him, he wanted to kill him. The mark of shame truly evoked the greatest anger in everyone, regardless of which side they were on.

Matteo was good, and a few times he almost wiped Ben with the blade. Ben kept managing to dodge the blade, which seemed to buzz with every attempt to stab and cut.

Finally, Ben managed to block one of Matteo's attacks and kick him in the right knee. Matteo cried out in pain and Ben rammed his own knee into his side, immediately twisting his arm so that the Italian had to give up his blade. When Ben also pulled his leg to the side, Matteo went down. However, he did this next to the pistol he had just dropped.

Before Matteo could grab it, Ben grabbed the knife and jumped to the side as Matteo also fired his first bullet in his direction, tearing a hole in the bark of a tree.

"Not bad for a nobody!" Matteo said with a sneer. "Truly, we would have had less problems with the Turk."

Matteo let his pistol circle, aiming at no particular target. He couldn't see much through the darkness, either. Carefully, he reached into his jacket with his free hand and pulled out a full magazine. In a flash he had removed the almost empty one and replaced it with the new one. Only then did he reach for one of the flashlights lying on the ground, whereupon he crossed his hands and thus always shone in the exact direction in which he was aiming.

"Okay, this makes it a lot more fun!" he said. "I love it when my victim balks or runs away. It makes a fight like that so much more exciting. I admit to underestimating you. It won't happen to me again!"

He waved the flashlight around, thinking he heard something, but he was professional enough that he didn't just shoot. His senses were so heightened that they automatically reacted to typical outlines. Here in the forest, however, his senses and instincts were challenged to the utmost. Moreover, it was pitch dark and only the flashlights of the four dead Russians provided some additional light.

Matteo had to admit to himself that this was truly not his terrain. He was more interested in sneaking into houses or parties and events. But in the middle of the forest? That was not his thing. But he was adaptable. Always had been.

He had recognized early on how things really worked in his world. His father saw it differently and his mother also tried again and again to persuade her son. Matteo realized that life on a farm was not for him. To toil day after day in the vineyards, while the sun burned down on him, year after year – no. He would rather be one of the people who were able to live in the world. He preferred to be among those to whom his father and his family brought the wine. To whom he bowed and showed respect. And feared.

These people never worked in the vineyards. They sat in the shade in front of their magnificent houses and wanted for nothing. And they drove expensive cars that gleamed in the sun. They did not know money worries and took care of everything.

Matteo was not stupid. He knew what they were and what they did for a living. Unlike his father, however, he was not afraid to tell them exactly when they asked him about it. And he knew that one way out of his already prescribed life was through them. Into a life that offered him everything he only wanted. This had its price, and Matteo was ready to pay it. Thus, he did everything that was asked of him. He never had to be asked twice.

Or they didn't even do that, because Matteo instinctively knew what was expected of him. That's what gave him a good life. And respect. So much respect that he was sent here alone, even though they knew he could meet several men. They didn't do that because they wanted to send him into a trap or use him as cannon fodder. No. They knew they could rely on him. If even one had guessed... But that was another story he would help clear up. Maybe it really was time. But there was only one thing standing in the way of all that, the big plans, now. And Matteo would not allow that to happen.

Matteo continued to move forward, peeking behind each tree as he felt his tension steadily rising. This Ben was not just anyone, and certainly not a nobody. He should have killed him directly, but now it was too late. And it would cost him time. Time he didn't have. He should have been in another place long ago.

"I'm already investing way too much time in you. We should end this now!"

"Whatever you say!" a voice suddenly rang out, sending Matteo scurrying. There he stood. Ben.

Matteo pulled the trigger. Once. Twice. Three times. But no bullet hit Ben. At least Matteo couldn't see it.

But he must have hit him. Three shots? One must surely have hit his target.

Cautiously, Matteo moved forward. Slowly. Feeling too safe could very quickly lead to himself lying bleeding on his back. He was sweating. He hadn't done that for a long time. He felt the adrenaline rushing through his body and he did not like this feeling at all.

He had not had an opponent like Ben for ages. A real opponent who challenged him. Actually, he should avoid such situations. Finish them off like he did with the four guys. He knew that they would not cause him any problems. But Ben...

Blood. There was blood on the tree. So he had gotten Ben. How big the wound was, he couldn't say, but at least Ben was hurt now. That was at least something, even if Matteo had hoped to find him lying here.

A crash made Matteo turn around. He just saw the last of the flashlights of the now dead men go out, plunging everything into darkness. Now his own flashlight was the only one left burning. There was no other source of light.

He was starting to feel queasy. He had already competed against men who had a lot going for them. Sometimes it was a matter of taking out someone who was basically the same as he was. It was a duel at eye level, which Matteo always enjoyed. But he had never encountered anyone like Ben, with whom he increasingly had a very bad feeling. He just couldn't judge him and wished he had had more information about him. To be able to proceed as he normally did, by first making inquiries and studying his victim closely.

This would have been more than helpful with someone like Ben. Then this all would have gone very differently.

Had Ben only destroyed the flashlights or had he also taken any weapons? Matteo did not know with certainty what weapons the Russians were armed with, but assumed that there were also some firearms. Ben definitely had a knife, but what else did the four men themselves have with them? They certainly hadn't been here without guns. If Ben now had a firearm as well...

Matteo had to leave. He had already wasted too much time here. That had not been his mission. But like so many things in this night, some things had not gone according to plan. On the other hand, he couldn't afford to let Ben get away either. The danger of suddenly having him at his back was simply too great. He had to catch him.

Something jumped out from behind a tree directly in front of him. A figure, unmistakable.

Matteo fired. And this time he hit. He fired again and again and again. Each shot was accurate. He could see the blood and how the body shook under the bullets.

At the fifth hit, Matteo realized he had made a mistake.

By then it was too late.

He had just the chance to turn his weapon in the right direction when Ben was already standing in front of him, deflecting the barrel of the weapon away from him with one hand and ramming the knife diagonally upwards into Matteo's body with the other and twisting it immediately. Matteo was dead on the spot and fell like a wet sack next to the corpse of the

Russian, whom Ben had stripped of his jacket and shirt and used as bait.

Ben looked down at Matteo, whose frozen eyes were illuminated by the flashlight. Then he picked up the flashlight and looked at the wound on his left side. A bloody line stretched along it. A few inches more inward and he would truly have had bigger problems and would probably have been the one lying on the ground.

Finally, he shone the light on the bodies. A moment ago, he had only wanted to get the flashlights out. Now he examined them to see if the men had had any weapons with them, which was indeed the case. Each of them had a firearm and several magazines. They also had brass knuckles and knives.

Of all of them, Matteo had the most similar stature to Ben. Unfortunately, he had ruined his clothing, so he had to make do with something less suitable. At least it was black.

He also found a car key on Alexei's body, as well as on Matteo's. With any luck, he would have a car, which also meant he would find a first aid kit there. He had truly had worse wounds, had had to endure more pain, but he also knew that such a wound could quickly turn into something worse.

But this would not happen immediately. A basic cleaning would have to suffice, as he had something much more important to do. He had to find Anna.

13

The icy rain pelted down. Mercilessly. It was freezing cold. And the wind only made things worse.

Finn stood bare-chested and shivering. His limbs felt frozen, but unfortunately it didn't numb the pain of the cold.

Finn staggered, but he did not fall. Not even when Erik's blow struck him in the head against his left temple, as Erik had immediately seen Finn's inattention and sensed an opportunity. The hit was hard and someone other than Finn would have surely have been to the ground. Finn, however, merely stumbled back, but did not go to his knees.

What was still keeping him on his feet, no one could say. The other boys, standing spellbound around the battlefield, had also lost all sense of time. No one was doing their own exercises or fighting anymore. Even the teachers were standing there watching Finn fight his sixth opponent.

He had knocked the first three unconscious. Then Odin had sent two directly against him, who fared no better. Matt and Erik had lasted the longest so far, mainly because Finn had been on the training ground since early morning, while they had only arrived at the usual time.

Erik followed suit, paying no attention to Matt, who by now seemed to be stirring again. He knew he had Finn, and he smiled inwardly. Finn might have proven that he could take a lot, but now his strength was visibly failing him. It was only a matter of time now before Erik would knock Finn to the ground, to Odin's satisfaction.

Ever since the incidents when Finn had not only refused to kill his dog, but had also tried to save a nigger, Odin had been anxious to get Finn back on the right track, even if it killed him. Everyone knew that Odin still thought Finn was a great fighter who merely lacked the right attitude. Either Finn finally took his place, or he would die.

Finn's stance was unsteady. And his hemp-laced hands were shaking. He had a laceration over his right eye that was bleeding badly. So did a cracked lip and various bruises that were easy to see. But just as plain to see was what a muscular body he possessed. Yes, he would certainly make a perfect warrior one day, if he didn't die first. Perhaps it would be Erik who now brought him death.

Again and again Erik struck at Finn, who by now could block his blows only inadequately, and hardly made any attacks himself. Erik really had him in the palm of his hand, controlling him and the fight. But battered opponents were dangerous, Erik knew that. Finn especially was not to be underestimated. Maybe today was the day when Finn really had nothing left to oppose. Maybe everything ended today, just as Finn had overcome Gunther. The invincible defeated. Maybe today was the day when finally, he, Erik, would gain the recognition of the community.

Erik allowed himself a smile, feinted with his left shoulder, and with his right arm lashed out to give Finn a blow so violent that he could no longer intercept it.

Erik's fist shot forward like a thunderclap. He put all his strength into it, his whole body. Finn would feel like he had been hit by an anvil, if he felt anything at all after the hit.

With that fist and a similar blow, Erik had not long ago simply killed a member of an inferior race who were here to take their land and their way of life. Of course, this was different because the inferior races did not have the same physical constitution as they did and were therefore easier to kill, but nevertheless it had earned him the mark that he now proudly wore on his left forearm.

He even had the same symbol tattooed on the left side of his chest that adorned the left side of Finn's chest. Erik wore it, however, not out of shame, but as confirmation that he belonged to this community. He felt that he belonged to it and to it alone. It was his confession that he had nothing in common with the people out there and that he belonged to his community. His pledge.

Which sign would he get if he killed Finn now? Would Odin then choose him as a new protégé? As a candidate?

All this went through Erik's mind in a fraction of a second as he delivered his killing blow. In the same thought, he could already feel his fist hitting Finn's face. How the nose broke in a shower of blood. The jaw. The cheekbones. Teeth breaking off or coming loose. Everything turning into a bloody pulp. The skull splintered and rammed into the brain.

But Erik's blow was never to reach Finn's face.

From one moment to the next, Finn's stance had been firm again, his trembling over and his gaze focused. He dodged to the side, deflecting Erik's blow so that he in turn could ram his elbow into his face and his knee into his stomach. Since Erik was in forward motion and focused only on his punch, it was too late for him to defend himself or tense his muscle. Thus the hits were amplified.

Already, more blows were hitting Erik, rocking his world. Instinctively, he executed the defensive modes he had trained in for so long, which simply went off without any thought, but were inconsequential here and now. Finn blocked them all, only to apply more hits and finally wrap his arms around Erik's neck. Now it was easy for him to either break his neck or deflate him. Or both.

"Stop! Stop struggling!"

Erik only heard the words from kind of far away and then again up close, since Finn's head was right next to his.

"Give up!"

No retreat. No surrender. No mercy.

Giving up was not an option. They had learned that from childhood. It had been literally drilled into them. How many times had he been in unspeakable pain and still had to keep going. Training his body. Doing the never-ending exercises. In preparation for the great day when the warriors and especially the Deathbringers would give everything back to the people. The great day when they would restore the old order, this time for good. Only the bravest and toughest would endure and prove themselves worthy.

No retreat. No surrender. No mercy.

"Give up!"

"No!"

Finn had him. As hard as Erik tried, Finn had a firm grip on him. He had aimed his punches right at Erik's muscles, so they were now refusing to do their job. Erik couldn't reach for Finn either, as Finn knew very well how to maintain his better position.

Erik clawed his fingers, his nails into Finn's arms, but Finn would not let go. Even when he felt Finn's warm blood running down his fingers, Finn didn't let go.

And then Erik felt his senses fading more and more. Desperately he tried to find a foothold with his feet. But the ground was far too muddy from the constant rain. In addition, they lay, he on Finn, who had thereby the better position.

The world around Erik became first blurred, then darker and darker.

"Break his neck!" Erik heard a voice that seemed to come from far away. Odin.

Then Erik's senses faded completely. Just before it went black, he heard only one word.

"No!"

Then his world finally went dark.

14

When Anna opened her eyes, she knew that something had gone wrong. Just a moment ago she had been in the forest and now... Yes, where was she?

Her eyelids were heavy and her head hurt. She closed her eyes and tried to remember what had happened.

Ben.

Ben had been with her and had taken her to the forest because he thought they would be safe there. He had been able to read Mo's code, which probably made him the only one.

She shook her head.

And then Russev's men had shown up. It had to be them. Before she could understand or say anything, one of the men had knocked her down. And now here she was. Tied to a chair in a dirty, once white-tiled room with old pipes running through it. Everything was old and looked ready for demolition. Only the long neon tubes were new and bathed the room in a threatening, cold light. Just the impression of the surroundings sent a cold shiver down her spine.

Anna knew where she was. She had heard about this before. The old sugar factory, which had been empty for ages and for which there was no buyer. Or rather, there should be no buyer. Because Russev had a great interest in continuing to use these premises.

Buying the property would have been too conspicuous for him. So the factory remained in the possession of the bank. Any buyers were deterred by the fact that remodeling or removing the old masonry would require large investments. In addition, there were expert opinions that suggested that demolition would cause major environmental damage. Unauthorized material would have been used. All this was enough to keep most of the willing buyers away without any problem. For the stubborn ones, however, Russev had his own methods.

Now she, too, had landed here. And she knew only too well that she would only get out of here alive if someone came to her rescue.

She could not expect this from the man who was tied up next to her. Ahrend certainly looked much worse than she did. He was bleeding from a wound on his forehead and lip. His undershirt was stained with blood, as were his pajama pants.

Anna screwed up her face. Then she looked around. There had to be a way to escape, or everything would only get much worse.

The chairs could be moved, but both she and Ahrend had been attached to them with cable ties. They wouldn't be able to get them open. And if they fell over by trying too hard, they would surely break many a bone.

On the table in front of them, their backpacks had been cleared out. Everything was still there, which was at least something. Whether it was of any use to her, she could only hope.

How much time had passed?

And how thick were the walls?

And the steel?

She wasn't in a basement, if she looked closely. Or was she?

Would there be a signal through here...?

Footsteps that were getting louder and louder were approaching them fast.

Now it came down to this. At least she had to buy some time or better.

She could already tell from Russev's face that he was not pleased. With him were some of his men, all of whom would do whatever he asked at a hint from him.

Russev smiled menacingly as he looked at Anna. "Ah, Mrs. Kerkov. How nice. You're already awake."

With that he nodded in Ahrend's direction and one of the men walked up to him to slap him hard across the face with the flat of his hand. This had the desired effect and Ahrend cried out.

The next moment another man came and poured an eggmer of water on Ahrend, which finally brought him round.

"What the hell...?!" he gasped. But then he remained silent, as he grasped the situation with a few glances. Then his face turned white as a sheet. "Have you lost your mind? What is this shit now?"

Russev didn't let that rattle him. "Ah, Mr. Ahrend also honors us. How nice that we meet in person."

Anna's blood froze in her veins. They were as good as dead.

"What's this all about?" Ahrend finally followed up. "Why am I here?"

Russev acted surprised. "Why are you here? Because shit is flying around our ears! Because you messed up big time! *That's* why we're here!"

Russev stood up from the table and shook his head. "Everything was going great, only then you got too greedy, didn't you? Do you think we wouldn't notice your side businesses?"

He walked up close to Ahrend. "Of course we did. But it didn't matter much as long as our employees were happy and it didn't get in the way of our business. Everything was fine. But then you became too greedy and, above all, too careless. And all of a sudden your activities threatened to be exposed, which also put our business in danger. And what did you do?" Russev snorted and spread his arms. "Well, there you see where that led."

Russev stroked his face. "It took me years to build up my business. And in one night, everything threatens to collapse. Just like that. But you're finally going to correct that, Administrator!"

With that, he glared at Ahrend as if he wanted to peel the skin off his bones with his gaze alone.

Ahrend smiled arrogantly. "You set it all up? Honestly? Who really turned what you built into money? And gave everything a veneer of legality, so to speak? If it weren't for me, you'd be just another temporary gangster."

Russev struck. Hard, so that blood immediately spurted from Ahrend's nose and even splashed Anna.

Ahrend's face turned almost as red with anger as it did from the blood. "You stupid asshole! You..."

"Don't you dare do that again!" Russev said. "My patience has been tested long enough!"

Just then, a man came and placed a laptop on the table.

Russev's eyes remained fixed on Ahrend. "I know you're both involved in this, and I'm sure Ms. Kerkov can be of assistance if you're not."

Ahrend's eyes grew wide. Russev might get the idea that he didn't need him anymore. But that lasted only a moment. Then he laughed derisively again.

"Her? Why her?"

Russev looked at Anna. "Can you fix it?"

Anna swallowed. "If I have full access to the files..."

"And she doesn't have that," Ahrend grinned. "Only I have that."

Russev smiled. "That's good to know. So why didn't you do anything about it? Weren't you going to send your men out and take care of it?"

Ahrend looked at Russev in irritation. "My men?" Then he laughed. "Yes, that fits. After all, it's me who pays them. After all, I manage all the money."

Russev smiled. "Yes, however, you manage it. More than was actually intended, wasn't it? Don't you have a lucrative side business going with Sergey? Isn't he also in your service, supplementing his coffers a bit?"

Ahrend's eyes flashed and Russev's face got a little wrinkle of anger on his forehead. "And do you think you could threaten me with them? Sergey may do business with you too, that's okay. But he couldn't protect you when my men, who are subordinate to me and *only* me, dragged you here. And Sergey couldn't help you either when it came to eliminating the problem."

Russev closed his eyes. "This ends today and here. You will fix all this and then we will part ways. Forever."

Ahrend was so perplexed that he could only nod. Russev nodded as well, stepped aside and pointed to the laptop.

"Then please."

Ahrend swallowed again and looked helpfully at Anna, who also just looked at him, frightened.

"It can't be done from here," Ahrend tried to explain.

Russev laughed. "Don't worry about the connection. It's top-notch here."

Ahrend shook his head as if he were dealing with a silly little boy. "All the files are on the computer at the branch. But on top of that, there's no connection. You have to get to it to be able to do anything."

Because Russev's gaze became piercing again, Anna nodded. "He's telling the truth. For all safety, everything is stored only there and can be changed only from there."

Ahrend smiled with disdain. "Do you think I'm stupid enough to make the files accessible to everyone? It might be a little inconvenient that way, but it's also much safer. Always has been."

Russev looked at him. Anna realized that he would like to punch Ahrend again, but held back. As long as he didn't know if he didn't really need it, he had to practice patience. And it wouldn't help her if she affirmed that she could manage everything just as well as Ahrend, even better. Right now, as much as she couldn't grasp this, Ahrend and his, as always, shitty behavior was the best way to ensure the survival of them both. The night had gone so disastrously that Russev could not afford any more mistakes. From that point of view, everything could still turn out for the better. With a little luck, it would be all over tonight.

Russev finally nodded, appearing again like the sympathetic nice Russe that perhaps he really was in the right situations. "All right. Then we'll go to the branch."

Anna bit her lip, but then spoke. "Isn't it under surveillance?"

Russev looked at her with a look as if he were looking at a cockroach. For a brief moment he was silent, seeming to consider whether to answer her, the woman at all. "That's settled. There will be no police there."

Ahrend smiled wryly. "And then? What's going to happen then?"

Russev's eyes flashed. "They'll take my money away and erase all the clues and data on the computer. Because the police will show up. Not now. But during the course of tomorrow, for sure."

Then he spread his arms. "Instead, cheer this Turk up and make it all look like he embezzled. I don't care how you do it, but there should be no more reference to me or your side businesses there. We'll see how it goes from there. Let the grass grow over it. Who knows. But for tonight, I want everything out of here. Got it?"

Ahrend took a breath and shook his head. Then he snorted contemptuously.

He was about to say something when everyone heard audible noises.

Anna listened. Yes. Unmistakable.

"What's that?"

Ahrend laughed and shook his head again. "Well, fabulous. I always thought you were more subtle than that."

Anna saw how Russev's words infuriated Ahrend, but he held back. Unless Ahrend had another ace up his sleeve, Russev would surely kill Ahrend today, once he had done what Russev wanted. Anna just had to make sure it didn't hit her too and take the chance when it did.

Russev walked over to one of his men and whispered in his ear. "Contact Sergey."

The man hesitated. "Is that wise?"

Russev slapped him against the chest. "Are you going to tell me what is smart and what is not? He started this shit, then let him finish it. I want him here. Now! And tell me what the fuck is going on!"

Anna had a hunch.

Ben watched the factory. He still knew it from the time when it was in operation. But that was not for long. And when it was shut down, it was of course the perfect place for young people to retreat, have unsupervised parties and engage in tests of courage. For Ben, above all, it was a retreat where he could also train in peace and quiet, just as he had always learned to do.

He didn't need any expensive, special training equipment to do this. He trained alone with the help of his own body weight. This did not isolate individual muscles, but trained them together, in correct movement sequences. This helped him to remain more supple in his movements, which made him move as naturally as possible during his *parkour* runs through the factory grounds.

Mo had always called him crazy. He preferred the ambience of a gym, which also gave him the opportunity to pick up girls. But Ben didn't feel like doing that, which Mo had never quite understood.

Ben had been here many times and knew the whole place like the back of his hand. It was also unlikely that anything had changed over the years, with the exception that there were now some men wandering around, armed, and looking as if they were guards.

Ben had been surprised to actually find several cars when he left the forest. Matteo's car proved to be the least conspicuous, being an older Golf, where one had to look several times to see that the facade did not match the interior.

In the trunk, Ben also found an unopened first aid kit, which he used to care for his wound. This would be fully sufficient for the next few hours, so he would not have to worry about it until he had freed Anna.

He would have preferred to drive directly to the factory at full speed. But this would have attracted too much attention. He decided to park the car at a safe distance and then set off on foot.

Once he had established that he was most likely in the right place, he crept up cautiously. The compound was not exactly small and the buildings large and winding. Anna could be held anywhere. There were no clues as to where.

Taking out each of the guards one by one if possible still seemed like the most feasible course of action, except that it wouldn't get him to Anna fast enough. Who knew what kind of person this Russev was and what he intended to do with her?

Ben looked around. What options did he have? Finally, a risky plan developed in his mind, which spoke against everything he actually wanted to do. But it was the only solution. And perhaps a huge mistake.

He waited until he spotted some of the guards. Then he fired far away next to them. Immediately, all sorts of firearms were swung in his direction.

Ben visibly tossed his weapons away.

"I'm unarmed!" he shouted. "And I have information for Russev that I'm sure he wants to hear!"

Then he stepped out from his cover with his hands up.

Russev looked at Ben and looked him straight in the eye. "So you're the one who is causing us so much trouble," Russev stated. "You and that Turk. Quite amazing."

Ben remained motionless, simply looking straight ahead. The men had taken him straight to Russev and, as he had hoped, Anna was with him, unharmed. She looked at him with a stunned expression, as if he were a ghost.

Ahrend narrowed his eyes. "Aren't you the guy who was going to apply for a job with us? Ben Becker or something?"

Ben remained unmoved as Russev looked back and forth between him and Ahrend. Then he laughed. "Another banker like that? And you killed all my men? Man, you guys seem to be learning very different stuff in your banker school than I actually suspected. What good is that? In a bank robbery? Can you go Bruce Willis and kill everybody? I'm impressed."

Russev threw his arms in the air, then exhaled in resignation. "Maybe this is all a sign that I should retire." He shook his head. "Sergey, put him down. But nice and slow, I want him to get something out of this and bitterly regret ever getting in our way. By doing that, you might make up for some of the mess we have here because of you, too."

The man smiled. His wounds had been treated and bandaged, but you could clearly see that Mo had taken a lot out of him. "Then I will kill at least one of you tonight. After all, your friend had refused to die. He put up a brave fight and really surprised me. Tough guy. He just wouldn't give up. Heard it took several bullets to finally take him down."

Ben's eyes glinted with anger and he clenched his fists.

Russev shook his head. "Under different circumstances, I'd like to see the fight. Sergey against someone who wants to avenge his friend – that sounds promising. Unfortunately, we don't have time for that. So just finish him off."

Sergey smiled and was about to walk towards Ben when Anna cried out.

"You can't kill him!"

Russev showed surprise. "Why not?"

"There's a cell phone. There could be evidential material on it, and he hid it."

Russev looked at Ben. "Is that so? Interesting." Then he looked back at Ahrend. "You see? That's what I mean. Everything has become totally complicated. All it took was a cell phone, and already your computer, which isn't connected to anyone else, is worth nothing."

Then he turned to Ben. "You haven't made any copies, have you?"

Ben's expression remained unchanged. "There's only the cell phone. Mohamed Aslan handed it over to me. There is evidence on it that links Ahrend to you."

Russev took a breath. "Of course. I guess it wouldn't do any good to torture you into telling us where that cell phone is."

"I'd like to try," Sergey agreed. "Or we could torture the bitch."

Anna looked in horror at Russev, then at Ben, and finally at Sergey.

Russev looked at Sergey as well, then waved him off before turning back to Ben. "No. This is all taking too long. I mean, I don't like such methods. Sometimes I have no choice. You have to show strength, you understand.

"I have my men for dirty work and stuff. Sergey here. But I actually have them so I don't have to use them. As a deterrent. That kind of thing helps. Well, there are some stubborn ones, you do have to let them off the leash, but not that often." With that, he pointed at Ahrend. "Our friend here had quite different plans. I never liked them, but unfortunately, I let it happen. That was my mistake and now I have to pay for it."

He took a breath. "So how can we shorten this thing?"

"I just want Anna. Her and my life against the cell phone."

Russev nodded. "That's a good match. I had plans for her anyway, assuming she stays alive. That brings us to you. You are an interesting young man with many talents. Talents to make things difficult for me once again. But also talents that could prove useful. So I am very much inclined to take you up on your offer."

Ben looked Russev in the eye. Then he nodded.

Russev laughed and patted Ben on the shoulder. "Very good. Then let's see about getting to that damn computer so we can finally put this whole business to rest."

Ahrend looked angrily at Russev. "And what about me?"

Russev acted surprised. "What about you?"

"Well, I'm part of the deal, aren't I? If you have the phone and I've done everything like you said, I get to go too!"

Russev gritted his teeth. Then he nodded in Sergey's direction. He approached Ahrend and pulled out a knife.

"Hey, what the fuck?" shouted Ahrend, looking back and forth between Sergey and Russev in disbelief.

"But just a lesson," Russev said, and Sergey turned Ahrend's right hand around and cut across his palm. Ahrend cried out loudly, to which Russev shook his head in annoyance. Immediately Sergey put the knife to Ahrend's throat, whereupon the latter fell silent.

"He likes it quiet."

Ahrend bit his lip and then nodded. Sergey cleaned the blade on Ahrend's undershirt and put the knife away and his hands in his pockets as he stepped aside again.

With an expression between anger and pain, Ahrend looked at his hand with blood running down it. "Shit, how am I supposed to type now?"

"Oh, I think Mrs. Kerkov can certainly help with that," Russev replied. "Just think of it as familiarization. And if you do everything to my satisfaction, then maybe I'll refrain from allowing Sergey to cut you into little slices, starting with her tail."

Ahrend looked at Russev and for the first time Anna really recognized uneasiness in him.

"What is that?" suddenly one of Russev's men said, pointing to a small square object on the table. This had begun to vibrate and a narrow light had come on at the top. Russev lifted the object and looked at it with amusement. Since it was obviously from Anna's backpack, he held it out to her.

"What is this? A pocket bomb? Am I not allowed to let go of this now or I'll blow up?"

Anna smiled. "No. This is a pager."

Russev smiled. "Cute. It says 'ready to go.' What does that mean? Is there a police task force waiting outside?"

Russev laughed. His men, except for Sergey, did the same.

Anna smiled. "Police? No, I don't think so. If you would press the button, please."

Russev raised his right eyebrow in surprise. He kept his eyes on her. "Boris? Gun!" He ordered, without taking his eyes off Anna, who met his gaze.

Boris handed the pistol to Russev, who pointed it at Anna. She continued to remain unimpressed. "I hope for your sake that no police show up here in a minute."

Russev pressed the button.

Nothing happened.

Everyone listened, but nothing could be heard.

Anna continued to look Russev in the eye.

Inaudible to most, Ben heard a noise.

When the head of his guard exploded to his right, he dropped to the ground. By then the face of another was torn away and blood splattered everywhere.

Ahrend screamed. "What the fuck is this!"

Two more of Russev's men went down, hit by multiple bullets.

Russev looked around and saw Sergey pointing his pistol, smoking from the silencer, at him with a smile. Russev looked at Sergey in disbelief, then back at Anna. Anna smiled as well. Russev's face turned red.

"You...!"

Before Russev could pull the trigger, he felt the hot silencer of Sergey's gun near his forehead. Sergey stood beside him smiling and shook his head to put his free hand on Russev's gun and take it from him.

"Sergey, what are you doing?" hissed Russev, but otherwise did not move.

Sergey shrugged his shoulders. "As they say here: *Whose bread I eat, whose song I sing.*"

With his hands raised, Russev walked back. His eyes glinted and remained fixed on Sergey. "How could you? I trusted you!"

Sergey kept the pistol pointed at Russev. "That's right. But the Administrator simply made me a better offer. As you said, men like me only serve as a deterrent. But on the free market my skills are in great demand. I also have to think about my future. And I see it somewhere else. So does everyone."

Russev looked at Ahrend. "You dirty asshole!"

Ahrend looked back in amazement. "Hey, I don't know what this guy is talking about. I invested some money for him and others without clearing it with you, yes. But what fucking contracts he's talking about, I don't know. What the fuck is going on here?!"

Sergey smiled and went next to Anna's chair. There, without taking his eyes off Russev, he bent down and cut Anna's bonds.

Smiling, Anna stood up and rubbed her wrists.

"What the fuck is this?!" hissed Ahrend again.

Russev's eyes narrowed. "You're the Administrator."

"What?! No, no, no, *I* am! I've been managing all your accounts. The stupid bitch can't get anything done!"

Anna took a breath, picked up Sergey's knife, and without warning jammed it between Ahrend's legs. As he screamed, she looked deep into his eyes and twisted the knife.

"Tell me, how did it feel when you put your dirty hands on me? When you fucked me? Did it feel as good as this does now? Or is this as hot now as you always wanted it to be when you fucked my ass too?"

Anna raised the knife and rammed it between Ahrend's legs again. He screamed like a banshee.

"Do you still want to fuck me? In the ass again? Am I still making you horny now? You like a little pain, you said. But only when it affects others."

With that, she stood up and left the knife stuck between Ahrend's legs. She looked at Ahrend's pain for a while, then exhaled in resignation.

"Would you please take care of it?" she said and went to one of the dead men and picked up one of the pistols.

Sergey, meanwhile, went to Ahrend, not taking his eyes off Russev, pulled the knife out from between his legs, only to use it to slit Ahrend's throat.

Russev exhaled. "What the hell is this?"

Anna shrugged. "Consider it the end of our business relationship."

Before Russev could say anything, Sergey shot two bullets into his chest. Russev looked at him with a confused expression, then collapsed.

Anna pointed her pistol at Ben, who was still crouched on the floor with his hands up.

"Surprised?" asked Anna with a smile.

Ben shook his head. "I was thinking something like that. And Mo, too, I guess. Hence your name on the list."

Anna looked irritated. "*My* name?"

She picked up the list that was also on the table and studied it. Then her eyes fell on the last line and she smiled in understanding. "I guess it says more than just the path to the files."

She turned back to Ben, who just scowled at her.

"I suppose you want to know the reason why."

Sergey cleared his throat. "We should get out of here."

Anna glared at him angrily. "Scared because you killed your boss and the place is crawling with his men who don't react too well to that? I'll explain that shit to him. Thanks."

With that, she turned back to Ben, but waited a moment. "Do you know what that's like? No, not really. What it's like to come from the bottom? To not have a chance. Oh, you're always told you have a chance. You just have to try hard enough. You want me to tell you, I did. And what did it get me?

"I tried so damn hard, because I truly had the best motivation to get out of the dirty life. A life where my own father 'visited' me again and again at night, as he called it. *Little girl, I'm going to visit you again tonight. That's when you'll be nice to Daddy again.* Again and again.

"The worst was when he was drunk and lost control. I think he enjoyed it, which is why he faked the drinking. *Oh, sorry kid, but I was drunk. So you know that can happen.*

"But there was something good about his boozing. That's how I met a guy who was a regular at his games. And I found out what he did for a living. He was killing people for the Russian mafia. He didn't trust anyone, so he preferred to gamble away his money rather than invest it in any way.

"But when I started my banking apprenticeship, he approached me. He knew me and I knew him. I invested his money. In return, he killed my father. Slowly. He knew some really nasty guys who were into some really sick stuff. He gave my father to them. They were experts at torturing people and especially loved to rape their victims for hours with all kinds of objects. Every night before going to bed I would watch the episode of the day and it was a satisfaction.

"My father broke very quickly. He didn't have the strength of his little ones, who endured his repulsive touches for years. Finally, they just threw him into a basement room that had a camera with a live feed. So I could watch my father slowly starve to death. And my mother? I left her to the guys for nothing, just as she had simply left me to my father.

"Somehow word got around what I was doing for the guy, let's call him Yuri. As a result, others approached me and I invested their money. And my need to move up here in the bank wasn't so great anymore. Right here, in this sleepy nest, who would believe that money is laundered or even invested here for contract pilots? Only, Ahrend was on to me.

"The dirty pig couldn't take it that I didn't suck his cock at a meeting. He was not used to that. Each had sucked his dick. So he was looking for something to blackmail me with. And so he came across something.

"He may have been a scumbag, but unfortunately he wasn't stupid. A shitty combination. Especially for women who run into guys like that. Unfortunately, I couldn't dispose of him the way I did my fucking father, because he hooked up with Russev by stealing my idea. But I knew the time would come. And voila, it came. Though not in the way I intended.

"And now here we are, and you've really ruined everything. You piece of shit. Who are you? Mo always thought so much of you. But who you actually are, geez, no, not a dying word."

Anna paused and her features softened. "Mo was a really nice guy. I knew he had a thing for me. But just one little mention, one revelation of what had happened to me, and he left me alone. Oh, he flirted with me some more, but it was all subtle, friendly teasing, nothing more. So not at all what you should expect from the alleged Turkish machos. He was one of the good guys." She exhaled in resignation. "Too good, unfortunately, because he got the Ahrend thing. He wasn't wrong, but he should have stayed out of it. Unfortunately, he didn't and it all threatened to blow up. I couldn't let that happen. Neither could my clients."

Anna's eyes twitched and she clearly struggled to compose herself. "I will never again allow myself to get into a similar situation that I've been in before. I'm not going to prison. That's where my fucking father and my fucking mother would have belonged, but not me.

"I just did what I had to do to survive. I survived.

"I thought when I got rid of my father, it would be over. But it wasn't over. It went on. There were always men I had to be submissive to, so they didn't just destroy my career. I did it because I knew one day it would be over. If I didn't do it, it would be over right then and there."

She shrugged. "I should have stopped Mo before, then maybe it wouldn't have come to this. Should have gotten rid of Ahrend before and taken over Russev's affairs. Unfortunately, Mo got in the way, and then you. Jesus, you really made a stupid situation even shittier. Now I have to clean everything up and run. That was never the plan. But I'm going to rebuild my organization."

Anna laughed. "Shit, you'd make an excellent client. You've really got it together. But I don't assume you'd be interested. How would that look? I take on the guy who killed my clients? Bad for business.

"But I solved everything, and word will get out. People will be knocking on my door again soon enough. Maybe it'll revive my business too, who knows? I've always been very good at thinking positively, or I'd be dead by now."

She took a breath. "Whew, really felt good to get that off my chest. Talking doesn't actually help shit, but this really needed to come out because you were really getting on my nerves. Just killing you would have been just shit. I wanted you to know beforehand that you didn't fuck me. Nobody fucks me anymore. *Nobody* fucks me anymore. Not my father. Not all the other perverts who take advantage of their position. And not you either. I'll beat anyone. Cause I'm a fighter. I always get back up. Losers give up when they can't anymore.

Winners, when they have won. It won't be you who stops me from winning."

Her eyes glinted, but Ben just stared at her.

"Damn it, do you ever have anything to say?!" she snapped at him, but Ben's expression didn't change.

"You killed Mo."

Anna nodded, looking genuinely saddened. "But left you alive. Which was a huge mistake. I should have killed you back in my apartment. But I was still way too confused then, because shit just hit the fan over everything, and you informed me that Russev's men were after me. After that, everything suddenly happened so fast.

"I drugged you in the woods. I always have the injection with me when some shithead thinks he's going to assault and rape me. I thought that my people, whom I had called with the help of the pager, would then take care of you. But unfortunately, first Russev's people came instead."

Ben nodded. "Your killer came later. Matteo."

"Matteo? Now please don't tell me you killed that one too! Matteo was really cute."

"Matteo killed Russev's people and then I killed him."

She shook her head. "You bring death and destruction to all who deal with you. Just like you did with Mo."

She took a breath and all arrogance disappeared from her expression. "You probably won't believe me when I say this, but I really regret it. I wish he'd kept his hands off it. Then everything would have been fine. Ahrend would have disappeared sometime in the near future and I would have taken care of everything.

Everything would have been fine. Most of all, I never would have run into you."

"And technically, I guess I was the one who killed that Mo," Sergey interjected, smiling sardonically at Ben.

Ben's look at Sergey spoke volumes.

Anna rolled her eyes. "Had to do it now, huh?"

She looked at Sergey and took a breath. "Let me guess: You'd love to end this, too. And not by just putting a bullet in him. Shit, I should have shot him right then and there."

She raised her arms in resignation. "I'm going to get this all sorted out now and transfer all of Russev's accounts. Then I'll be on my way. You know where to find me. Do what you can't help doing and then join me. I'd recommend you just pick him off."

She turned to Ben and was silent for a moment. She smiled mirthlessly. "I really didn't want all this. I've made mistakes. I should have had Ahrend eliminated directly by my friends, but thought it was too conspicuous. He interfered. Blackmailed me and everything got out of hand. If Ahrend had been gone, I'm sure Mo wouldn't have noticed and none of this would have happened." Her face became serious again. "But I'm not going to let this ruin everything I've bled for."

Without giving him another look, she left the room.

Sergey and Ben looked at each other. While Sergey smiled and continued to point the gun at Ben, Ben's expression remained serious.

"So you killed Matteo, too," Sergey stated. "I don't want to say now that I liked Matteo, but I don't approve of it." He shrugged his shoulders. "I always assumed that he and I would work it out someday. Or we'd both grow old together somehow. But if we did, I would have taken it upon myself to kill him. And now I'm disappointed and curious at the same time."

Ben nodded. "So was Matteo. Now he's dead."

Sergey smiled. "Yes, the Italians. Can't let go of their machismo."

"Neither can you. Otherwise you would have killed me long ago."

Sergey nodded in agreement. "Yes, admittedly. You did kill Matteo, though. And many others. Some of whom I knew for a very long time. We were not unconditional friends. Good colleagues, you could say. They respected me. And you just killed them."

"They tried to kill me."

Sergey nodded slowly. "Yes, the old game."

Ben pointed at Russev and the other dead men with a nod. "You just killed your men, too."

Sergey shrugged his shoulders. "I guess I'm a bad person and I won't be the Colleague of the Month this time."

Ben waited. "So, what now?"

Sergey laughed. "Honestly, I don't really know either. How did you kill Matteo?"

"I stuck a knife in him."

Sergey laughed. "Matteo was good with the knife. Maybe as good as me." He nodded, then walked over to one of the bodies and pulled up the back of his jacket to reach underneath and pull out a knife. The black blade was a good twenty inches long, smooth in the front and serrated in the back.

"You guys are into army knives," Ben noted.

Sergey smiled and tossed the knife near Ben. Then he pulled out one of his own that could have come straight out of one of the Rambo movies.

"What can I say? Shoot someone, anyone can."

With that, he put the gun away and gestured for Ben to pick up his knife.

Slowly, Ben walked over to the knife and picked it up without taking his eyes off Sergey.

"I guess you showed your friend quite a bit," Sergey commented. "He really surprised me, I must admit. And the fact that he still held out, all the way home to himself, demands respect. You understand that it was purely business? He got too close. If Russev had discovered the extent of what Anna had set up there and he found out she was the real Administrator, well, he wouldn't have taken that well."

Ben nodded. "So Mo's death was purely business. For me, it was very personal. Your death will be very personal to me, too."

Sergey shrugged. "You should never take something like that too personally. It clouds your judgment and makes you unfocused."

Ben smiled weakly. "Then let's find out."

The two men got into fighting positions.

Sergey smiled and licked his lips in anticipation as they circled each other, waiting for the other to attack or if a gap could be seen, but neither gave an inch.

Sergey tried to move Ben in the direction of the bodies so that he might not pay attention and stumble over one of them. But it was as if he had a seventh sense, because he moved so skillfully that he avoided every tripping hazard. Sergey nodded appreciatively, then kicked the chair with the dead Ahrend, sending it flying in Ben's direction. Ben dodged out of the way. Immediately Sergey attacked, stabbed and missed Ben by a hair's breadth. Already he turned his knife around and stabbed again. Ben, however, had expected this, dodged, blocked Sergey's arm and cut across the jacket. But before the blade could touch the killer's skin, he dodged in his turn and got himself out of the danger zone.

Again the two circled each other.

Sergey raised the arm of the slashed jacket. "That one wasn't cheap. I'll chalk it up to teaching money."

He then attacked again, whipping his blade around and making Ben dodge again and again. Ben didn't even get to go on the attack himself and had to concentrate on Sergey and the surroundings at the same time. But it was also the environment that could help him.

Always use everything that is available.

Ben let himself fall backwards against the wall, but cushioned himself with one foot and then sped forward. Sergey could not cleanly execute his already planned attack as a result. Ben deflected Sergey's knife to the side and delivered a blow to his side. Sergey's face contorted in pain, but parried Ben's next advance and kicked him in the leg, throwing Ben slightly off balance. The result was a gash on his left shoulder.

"Oh, my knife tasted blood!" Sergey chuckled with a smile. "Now it wants more of it!"

Again he went on the attack. And now the blades clashed as well. Ben backed away and Sergey followed him, now leaving him no peace. Ben made better use of his free arm, so that again he managed to give Sergey another blow, which made him stagger to the side, whereupon Ben drew his blade across his back. This time he cut him.

Sergey dodged and gritted his teeth, then got back into position. "Now that hurt!"

With that, he reached behind him and pulled out another knife, this one slightly smaller. He grinned and attacked. His arms were like windmill wheels that Ben couldn't possibly escape in the long run. Sergey knew that. As far as fighting with knives was concerned, no one could fool him. Now Ben would also find out. There was no escape from him. He could not compete with him.

But Ben didn't want to.

He dodged, only to drop his knife and roll away to the side. Thereby he aimed at one of the dropped pistols and picked it up to immediately aim in Sergey's direction.

"Shit!" He shouted and jumped to the side so that the bullets flew past him. At the last moment he found cover behind an almost completely collapsed wall and drew his pistol himself.

"Pretty unfair of you!" he shouted at Ben, then pulled out a small radio.

"Everybody over here!" he shouted in Russian. "Russev and the others are dead!" Then he fired in Ben's direction. But he was long through the door.

"The perpetrator is still in the building!" continued Sergey. He followed Ben. Peering cautiously through the opening, he could see nothing.

"That bastard!"

Ben heard a general commotion. Voices seemed to be coming from everywhere and getting louder in his direction. He quickly hid in an alcove that was hard for anyone to spot, but he knew it was there. So he had a good view of the corridor, but no one saw him.

The men walked past him and Ben realized directly that there were too many of them. Russev must truly have ordered every available man to clear the situation. He had no chance against such an armed superiority. Here, after the announcement of Russev's death, each of them would pay attention to nothing and drop all restraint. If they spotted him, they would shoot at him with everything they had.

Sergey came out of the room, bloodied himself, and the men who looked in came out pale and full of anger. Sergey spoke to them partly in Russian. Ben could not understand everything. His knowledge of the language had already fallen asleep. The most important statements he understood in the end already.

The right weapons.

There had to be a hiding place here, where weapons were stored, which went beyond pistols and apparently obligatory army knives. Automatic weapons like machine pistols and rifles. His situation would not improve.

Ben needed weapons, too. More weapons than he had at the moment to stand against this superior force. If he fled now, his situation would hardly improve, because there were too many of them. Here, however, he knew his way around. Besides, he knew where he would find weapons here.

As soon as the factory was shut down, he had made it his retreat, his fortress. He knew that he could not simply discard his past. They would search for him, would hunt him down. To be able to escape then, or at least to have a chance, he prepared the factory area. It was unlikely that anyone had stumbled upon his hiding places by chance and that anyone here knew his way around as well as he did. That was his advantage.

Mo's father had always understood him. Knew about his worry and that it wouldn't leave him alone. And he knew that Ben would need guns. But they were not as easy to obtain in this country as in others. Aslan had gotten him weapons that were supposed to be destroyed. Ben had never asked how Aslan had done it, and Aslan had never told him. For a long time, Ben could not believe that a police officer would trust a young man he hardly knew and hand him firearms. Aslan had seen something in him and trusted him. He trusted that Ben needed all this and would not do anything with it that was not necessary.

Every now and then Ben had driven past the factory and had checked the locations. He had noticed that the factory had become busy again over time, but had not paid any further attention to it and had not visited the site again. In the meantime, he had regained so much confidence that this was no longer necessary. When the day would come, he knew that he would find everything as he had left it. Only he had never expected to have to go up against the Russian mob.

When the enemies outnumber you, what do you do?
Take them out, man by man.
And what is the most important thing to do?
Act from the shadows.

Aslan had gotten him guns that were used for hunting. Modified so that they caused greater damage and were therefore banned and confiscated by the police. These weapons had only one problem: they were very loud. Again, it showed how well Aslan understood Ben.

"You also need something with which you can be as silent as possible." With that, he took out a box and opened it. Looking inside then, Ben had to smile.

"Have you ever used something like this before?" Aslan wanted to know.

In response, Ben put the parts together, which elicited an appreciative smile from Aslan. It had always surprised Ben how wonderfully friendly, even warm-heartedly, this man could smile, who was otherwise so serious. And Mo had truly been his spitting image, like a younger edition, except that in time he had been able to shed his father's seriousness, though not entirely.

The box that Aslan had given him then was now Ben's foremost goal. Carefully, he slipped out of the alcove and looked around. He abandoned his plan to return to the room to help himself to the weapons there when he saw that there were two men there. He could not risk them noticing him and raising the alarm. One shot would be enough and he would face a superior force against which he could not stand.

Silently he moved away from the room and crept along the corridors. Again and again he heard voices and hid himself. Exactly because of such a situation he had chosen the factory as a precaution, in order to be able to retreat there if necessary. This was the ideal terrain, because it offered many possibilities to hide, but also to set traps for his opponents.

Fortunately, Ben did not have to go far until he reached the place where he wanted to go. It had been a long time since he had been here, and basically the small room with the old boilers, boxes and many pipes of different sizes had not changed. Sparse light fell through a broken window, but Ben did not need much. He knew exactly where to look and squeezed behind the equipment, then used various struts like wedges to climb to one of the topmost pipes where there was a hole.

Without making a sound, he retrieved a box. With it he climbed down and opened the hatch of one of the boilers to reach inside and pull out a canvas bag. He placed both on the floor and then, almost reverently, opened the box. It was all there. He had to smile involuntarily as he thought of how he had always felt when he had assembled the individual parts and then used it all.

Even before he joined Aslan, Mo and the family, he had watched movies. Movies had been a part of his education. Certain movies that had one thing as their theme: the truly limitless superiority of the white race portrayed in stories about heroes who usually took on superior numbers alone and were victorious. His favorite hero, then as later, had been John Rambo, who was not only an expert with firearms, but also with a more traditional one: the bow and arrow. Of course, Rambo's bow was not a traditional one, but a much more modern one, and Ben had always dreamed of owning one.

When Aslan handed him the box and Ben realized that it contained just such a bow, he knew that it was his favorite weapon ever. Exactly the one he needed now.

As if not a day had passed, he put the individual parts together and checked the tensile strength of the string, which was further enhanced by the pulley-like construction. With the appropriate arrow, such a bow had even more penetrating power than a rifle cartridge. An arrow was almost silent.

Ben opened the sack and took out a quiver of arrows, all of them provided with razor-sharp points consisting of three tapered blades. Of course, he didn't have arrowheads with explosives like Rambo had. But he had made some that did something similar, though not with as much explosive power. But he had other things for that.

Ben tucked his pistol into the back of his belt, strapped the quiver to his back, and attached three arrows to the bow's device. After hiding the sack and the box back in the cauldron, he set off.

The hunt had begun.

It took a little while before he encountered the first men, who by now had equipped themselves with automatic weapons. He could have shot them down with ease from his position. But he could not risk them firing a shot and thus revealed his position. Still, his tactic was to grab them one by one. But not yet. The time would come that required adjustment.

He moved almost silently through the maze of pipes and now useless machinery, taking advantage of every shadow, and waiting. Back when he had made the compound his own, he had explored every nook and cranny, and now he could move here as if he were a shadow himself.

The men had spread out everywhere. He probably could have left the compound unnoticed, but the danger was too great that they would then follow him.

A superior force in front of you is better than just one enemy at your back.

This was his compound. There was probably no one who knew his way around better. That was his advantage. Outside, it was a different story. The few men Russev had sent out had not been real opponents. They were better thugs. He could surprise them because none of them had been able to imagine that a single man could be dangerous to them and, moreover, fight back so mercilessly. They would not make this mistake. Even the way they held their weapons suggested that they had enjoyed many years of military training. That made them dangerous opponents.

Ben watched as two men with submachine guns searched the hallway. When they passed him, he slipped out of the shadows behind them, drew his bow and fired. The arrow pierced directly through the cerebellum of the man who had been hit and came out the front just below the nose. As the other man turned, Ben shot him an arrow in the eye.

Before going to them, he checked to see if there were others nearby. Since he could never make out anyone, he pulled the arrows out again and hid the bodies, including their weapons, in an adjoining room. He kept only one knife and some magazines. Then he crept on.

All the men Sergey had rounded up were now scattered around the compound, forming small groups consisting of a few men. That was what Ben had hoped.

When he encountered three again, Ben fired an arrow at a distant bucket. As it fell clattering to the ground, the three automatically oriented themselves in that direction, sneaking up until they were right in Ben's aiming line. Ben took aim and shot an arrow through two of the necks. As his comrades went down spitting blood, the third cried out in panic and spun around, searching. When he finally saw Ben, he aimed his machine gun at him. But before he could shoot, an arrow hit him right between the eyes.

Ben ran to the dead and took the arrows again, before he also shouldered one of the machine guns. He hastily hid – or half-hid – the three dead bodies.

He moved up the stairs to the roof of a building that had a small tower from which there was a good view over the area. This was an advantage, of course, but also a danger, since the tower could be easily targeted.

Ben looked through each of the broken windows and spotted isolated men as well as small groups. The factory was still surrounded by a high chain-link fence, complete with bell wire. It was impossible to get over there. Therefore, they guarded the exits.

Ben had no choice. He had to further reduce the number of his potential opponents and do so as quickly as possible, because he was running out of time.

He looked around and his eyes fell on the many parked cars near the factory's own gas station. When the factory was abandoned, they had emptied the tanks, of course. In addition, mainly diesel had been used at that time, which could be of little use to Ben in his plan. But maybe Russev had made the tanks usable for other purposes. This was quite the possibility.

Ben made a plan. It was risky, but he didn't have a better one.

Careful to stay out of sight of the men who were looking for him, he started to descend the stairs. Almost silently, he made his way down and walked through a corridor that even then had looked as if a bomb had hit it. For some reason, the young people here found it particularly fun to let off steam and immortalize themselves with graffiti.

Out of nowhere, a giant of a man appeared next to Ben with a rifle at the ready. Unlike the others, he had not gone in search of him, but had kept himself hidden so that he could ambush him. He had succeeded.

Immediately, Ben was able to knock the barrel of the rifle aside, but the giant struck directly, so that Ben had to drop his bow. As he reached for his gun, the man kicked Ben and slammed him into a wall. Ben used the impact to spring right back like a feather before his opponent could swing the gun in his direction.

Ben crashed into the man and they both went down. As Ben uncoiled, reaching for his pistol again and coming to a crouching stop, the man knocked the pistol out of his hand and executed a kick to his head that sent Ben crashing into a wall.

Reflexively, Ben raised his arms to protect himself from further blows to the head, but his body was uncovered. Immediately, his attacker's fist hit him, robbing him of his breath for a moment before the next kick hit him and threw him backwards. His back slammed hard against a concrete pillar and his senses faded for a moment.

When he looked back up, he saw the man truly towering over him, holding a walkie-talkie.

"I've got him!" he announced with a smile.

"Where are you?" Ben recognized Sergey's voice on the walkie-talkie.

Before the man could answer, Ben grabbed a loose stone and hurled it him. The man had to dodge, which gave Ben enough time to jump up and attack him directly. Immediately the man let go of the walkie-talkie to have both hands free.

Ben continued to throw blow after blow. However, the man was able to block and attack in his turn. He was strong. Very strong. An excellent fighter, whose attacks, bursting with power, Ben could only block and deflect with difficulty.

"You are good!" the giant said. "But I will break you for what you did to Russev and my comrades."

Ben took a breath and pulled out his quiver. "I guess it won't help if I tell you I didn't do this!"

The man snorted. "Of course not!"

With that, he attacked with even more fury, punching and kicking. His rage, however, made him unfocused and Ben kept finding a gap that he could use to place a hit. This only made his opponent angrier. His next blow was so powerful that it broke through Ben's guard and hit him in the stomach. Although Ben knew to put his arms up, it was too late and his opponent's knee slammed into his head.

Looking up from the ground, the giant picked up two short iron bars, cradled them in his hand and attacked. With full force, the iron bars hit the spot where Ben had been lying a moment ago. Again, he reached behind him, but his pistol sailed out of reach. Before any of the bars could hit him, he dodged and rolled.

Desperately, Ben looked around for a weapon. His eyes fell on his quiver of arrows. As the giant launched his next attack, Ben jumped to the side, rolled, then pulled out two of the carbon arrows. Holding one in each hand, he stood up. The giant grinned at him.

"You're good!"

Ben nodded. "You have no idea!"

With that, the giant attacked, striking with the iron bars, but Ben blocked them with the arrow shafts. Though the blows pelted down like windmill blades, Ben parried just as quickly, even managing to plant hits on his opponent. This only made the giant even more furious.

Ben skillfully dodged and the iron bars demonstrated their destructive effect when they hit the walls with full force, causing pieces to break off.

But even Ben could not avoid being hit. It was only thanks to his skill that he was able to get out of the danger zone as quickly as possible before he would have had to suffer worse injuries.

But then his opponent was so angry that he increased his speed. Ben would not be able to keep this up for long, as the skill and sheer power of his opponent would eventually bring him to his knees.

Ben turned the arrow over in his left hand. The tip of the arrow was now pointing down. On his opponent's next attack, he blocked the blow, only to have the sharp blades of the three-flighted arrowhead inflict cuts on him.

The man cried out and struck at Ben. He just managed to dodge, but stumbled and almost fell backwards, causing his opponent to immediately follow up. Ben, however, took the momentum and performed a backward roll, while the giant could not stop his onslaught. Ben stopped his roll, and when he came up, he rammed one arrow into the attacker's stomach and the other into his foot. The man cried out and struck at Ben, but he had long since dived back down and leaped toward his bow. Again he performed a roll, pulling an arrow from his quiver and putting it in immediately as he gripped the bow.

The giant realized what Ben was up to and didn't let his injuries stop him from charging after him. He raised his two iron bars to lunge for a mighty blow. Ben dropped to his back, pulled the string all the way through, and fired. The arrow entered under the chin of the giant, went through his head and came out on top, so that the arrowhead pierced deep into the ceiling, but the shaft was still in the head of the giant.

The iron rods fell clattering to the floor, while the man's body went limp and was only held upright by the arrow.

Ben took a breath and stretched. He felt the hits very clearly. At least one rib was cracked and the wound he had received from Matteo was bleeding again. Still, he didn't have time to concentrate on that. He gritted his teeth, strapped his quiver back on and picked up his pistol. When his eyes fell on the walkie-talkie, he picked that up as well and attached it to his belt. Finally, he picked up his bow and made his way stealthily further down.

The path to the parked cars offered some hiding places, but they did not completely protect him from being discovered. If someone looked down at just the right moment from a higher position, he would certainly discover Ben fast, and that would certainly have meant the end.

Cautiously, he crept to the parked cars, which once again indicated that there were some of Russev's henchmen here. He must have called everyone and apparently, due to the whole events, he did not care to protect the factory as his hiding place anymore.

Still watching for any movement, Ben went to the gas pump and took out the nozzle. When he turned it on, gasoline actually came out. Perfect.

Ben clamped the lever tight. Gasoline was steadily leaking out. He went to each car and cut the fuel lines so that a lake formed everywhere under the vehicles, connecting with the others.

Car by car, he moved forward, using them as cover, then continued to sneak.

Suddenly he heard a call. He looked in the direction from which it came and recognized three people on a narrow bridge near some boilers. Without delay, he took aim and fired an arrow. The one hit went down groaning, while the others refrained from raising their rifles and took cover. More arrows bounced off the iron railing.

When the men looked up again, Ben was no longer in sight.

Immediately, one of them pulled out his walkie-talkie. "He's by the cars!" he announced. "By the cars!"

Then he brought his rifle to bear and, with his comrades, crept cautiously along the walkway, finally making his way down a flight of stairs. All the while he kept his eyes on the cars, but could see nothing. Out of the corner of his eye he saw that more and more of his comrades were approaching and also setting their sights on the cars.

Sergey looked around, "Where is he? Find him, will you!"

All the men were running around looking into every car, but at the same time trying to be kind of careful, expecting that Ben could be anywhere.

Car after car was checked, the doors ripped open, as was every coffer space. Ben, however, remained missing.

"Where is he?!" shouted Sergey, visibly losing more and more of his composure.

"He *was* here," one of the men explained. "I saw him!"

"And why didn't you shoot him straightaway?"

The man backed away as Sergey approached him with an expression on his face that didn't seem to bode well.

"He shot at us with a... with a bow and arrow," the man said, weakly trying to defend himself.

That was the wrong answer. "*A bow and arrow?* And don't you have weapons? Guns? Then why don't you shoot back! He's got a freakin' bow and arrow!"

The man gulped.

"He destroyed all the cars," another suddenly declared, catching Sergey's attention.

"What?"

"Look. He cut the fuel lines. I guess we're not supposed to be able to track him."

Sergey looked at the man, then looked around. Saw the gasoline pump and the tap lying on the ground, from which gasoline was running steadily. The ground was already covered in gasoline...

"*Shit!*"

Then Sergey looked up and saw Ben rising some distance away, an arrow cocked in his bow.

When Ben let go of the string, Sergey jumped to the side. The arrow drilled into a hoop, which immediately went flat. Then the bow attached to it exploded.

The men screamed as almost the entire square turned into a sea of flames. Clothes caught fire on some, others tried desperately to stamp out the fire as it approached the cars, to no avail.

When the first car exploded, it started a chain reaction. The sea of fire became an inferno through which men staggered in flames or lay dead on the ground.

More explosions followed as the next cars blew up. Men came running, gazing in horror at the war-like spectacle unfolding before them. In panic, they shot at any hiding places they could make out. Others fled headlong, leaving everything behind.

As one man reloaded his gun, an arrow struck him squarely in the chest, pinning him to a pillar behind him. More panic broke out and the rest of the men shot in the direction where they thought Ben was. Shooting and screaming.

Slowly, Ben approached. He had put down his bow and replaced it with the machine gun. With it he aimed at the lying on the ground figures, but from these no more danger came. There was no one left to oppose him.

Sergey sprang up like the proverbial demon from hell and fired. Ben was jerked around as one bullet grazed his left arm and another bored into his leg. Falling, he just managed to take cover behind a pillar that protected him from the next shots. However, he had dropped his rifle.

Sergey staggered toward him, holding his weapon in front of him. His clothes, skin and hair were singed and partly burned. He had escaped the explosions only with great difficulty and now seemed to have trouble staying on his feet.

Ben leaned against the pillar and held his arm.

Sergey smiled mirthlessly. "Anna was right: I should have shot you right off! Way too much machismo!"

Ben nodded. "Yeah, she knew you wouldn't stand a chance!"

Sergey looked at Ben, then laughed. "Are you serious about this? You're coming with that now? You're appealing to my ego?"

Ben smiled weakly. "That's all you've got."

Sergey's eyes glinted. "You're down. I won." He grinned. "Like against your friend. He was good. Surprisingly good. But in the end, he got the feel of my knife. And I hurt him so bad with it that there was no saving him. I wanted him to perish slowly. Which he did."

Ben didn't let on. "But with Russev, you were more pragmatic. Just shot your comrades and then your boss. Apparently, you had been waiting for this for a long time."

Sergey took a breath. "That was part of the plan. We had to force-feed it and adjust it a bit. But yes, it was always part of the plan. And if you're wondering, I could just kill those: it wasn't that hard. I never had much to do with them. And Russev? He always treated me like his chain dog, scaring others with it. I only stayed with him because, well, money has to come from somewhere. But Anna showed me another way. And Russev was in the way. He wouldn't have approved. As I said with your friend, nothing personal. It was purely business."

Sergey's smile widened. "But killing you now is personal. I'm going to enjoy it."

Ben smiled. "I advise you to shoot me, as you did Russev and the others."

Sergey shrugged his shoulder. "That was purely pragmatic. I was looking forward to plunging my knife into Russev. But, after all, I wanted it to look like there had been a robbery. I had to improvise. But with you, I'll enjoy it all the more."

"You won't have much time for that. The police will be here any minute."

Sergey laughed. "Don't expect too much from them. *Whose bread I eat, whose song I sing.* If you know what I mean. I've always liked that saying. It's so clear, so realistic."

Ben nodded, looked past Sergey and his smile widened. Sergey looked at him in wonder.

"What's so funny?"

Ben pointed his chin at a vague point behind Sergey. He turned his head and recognized there three of the men who had just fled and were now scowling at him.

"You killed Russev!" one of the men stated. "And our comrades!"

Sergey glanced at them, then turned back to Ben. He lifted one of the walkie-talkies that he had taken from one of the men.

Sergey closed his eyes briefly, then nodded with a smile. "Not bad. Old school. Effective. Really not my day today. But it doesn't change anything."

The man in front of him snorted. "Yes it does, because now they're going to shoot you."

Sergey smiled. Then he turned abruptly and pulled the trigger before the men could pull the triggers of their weapons. One after the other, he fired several shots and kept firing even when the men were down. Only when he had made sure that none of them was moving did he realize that he had made a mistake.

Quick as a flash, he turned around. Ben punched his arm, causing Sergey's gun to fly out of his hand. Ben let his fist crash into his face.

Sergey went down and tried to get right back up. As he did so, he reached for one of the men's guns, but Ben was on him in an instant and stepped on his hand. Sergey cried out, rolled to the side and reached behind him. As he rose, he held his knife in his hand and looked down the barrel of Ben's pistol.

"I'm sure you know the saying," Ben commented.

Sergey's shoulders slumped powerlessly and he dropped the knife. "Never bring a knife to a gunfight." He paused for a moment. "I should have just shot you. And just killed your friend."

Ben shook his head. "You did kill him. Now get your phone out and unlock it."

Sergey laughed out loud, but did as instructed. "What are you going to do? Call the police? Please, I'd love to."

With that, he tossed the cell phone to Ben, only to immediately jump to the side, where there was another gun on the floor. Ben, his face contorted in pain, caught the cell phone and aimed it at Sergey before he could point his gun at him. Then he pulled the trigger five times, putting a bullet in each of Sergey's shoulders, knees and stomach.

Sergey collapsed screaming and remained shaking on the floor, unable to move, like a fish out of water.

Slowly, Ben came to him and picked up Sergey's knife. "There is a man facing you. He is your enemy. Then act accordingly. An enemy deserves no mercy."

He squatted down next to Sergey. "So if you have a chance to kill him, then kill him. If you can shoot him, then shoot him."

Sergey's eyes grew wide and he seemed to want to say something else, but Ben jammed the knife into his chest. Sergey's body went limp.

Ben looked at the lifeless body for another moment. The approaching sirens, however, jolted him out of his thoughts and he limped away to the last car, which had been parked off to the side and remained unharmed. He sat down in it and pressed some buttons on the cell phone so that it would not have to unlock.

When the first fire truck arrived, Ben blew open a side gate with his car. Now that he could be sure that no one else was going to stab him in the back, he had only one goal.

Anna.

And he knew where he would find her.

15

Finn ran as fast as he could. Faster than he could. Out-listing the guards had been the easiest part, but Odin had apparently expected him to escape. He had not been able to deceive him.

Finn had wondered all along why Odin hadn't just killed him. Killed him himself, because that seemed to be exactly what Odin wanted. They had all seen Odin break someone's neck for a lesser reason, or just beat them in a fight. Like Wolgar, who challenged him by questioning his judgment.

Wolgar was tired of waiting for the big day. Surely others were too, but Odin saw this as a good sign that the community was aware of their attention and burning for it. Wolgar, however, did not want to wait any longer. He did not think it was right to wait any longer, since the Verfassungsschutz was getting more and more on their trail. Already the killings of the last time had been too much. It was only a matter of time before the State Security would show up. So the order of the day for Wolgar was to strike now. It was the first time that a murmur went through the community, indicating approval.

Odin listened to Wolgar's words. He heard more and more voices agreeing with Wolgar. Then Odin nodded and stood up.

"So you disagree with my decision, Wolgar?"

Wolgar took a breath. "Your caution honors you Odin. But I think we must strike. If we wait too much longer, it may soon be too late."

"Are you calling me a coward?"

Wolgar contorted his face. "I would never do that. You are our Odin."

Odin nodded. "I am. And so this decision is mine to make. There is nothing more important to us than the great day. This is what we live for. This is what we are willing to give our blood for. If necessary, our lives."

"Without hesitation."

Everyone cheered.

Odin nodded. "I know that. But I am not willing to sacrifice their blood and lives for nothing. I am your Odin and you can expect me not to make my decisions lightly and not to send you into danger that could cost your lives without reason. That will be the case for one or the other on the great day. That's the way it's supposed to be. But they will fall, knowing that we will have the victory. Because it is the right time."

"So it shall be!" cried the community.

Odin stood up. "But you, Wolgar, say that I am not willing to put your lives in danger. That I shrink from sacrificing it for the right cause. That I am too weak to make that decision. I'm not. When the time comes, I will make the decision and I will bear the consequences. But to strike now would mean sacrificing the community. For nothing."

Silence. Everyone saw the blaze in Odin's eyes.

"You, Wolgar – you trained our warriors. You are the supreme of the Deathbringers. You know them best. Are they ready for the great day? Is our community ready? Will we be successful?"

All eyes rested on Wolgar. He looked around and tried in vain to hide how nervous he was. Nobody wanted to be looked at by Odin in this way. But then he moved his shoulders back and stirred his chin.

"Yes, they are ready. The time has come!"

Everyone cheered. Of course. To finally fulfill their calling to do what they had endured so much hardship and prepared for with complete conviction made them express their approval frenetically.

Odin smiled and raised his hand. Immediately they all fell silent.

"I have no doubt about the loyalty and willingness of every single person here to do exactly what we were born to do. And that's exactly why it's so important to take advantage of that and let them run to their doom. When everything is ready, they will fulfill their destiny, I have no doubt. But not until then. But the time is not yet. And I am not willing to sacrifice even one for your delusion."

"Delusion?!" exclaimed Wolgar, standing up as everyone else held their breath.

"That's right. Delusion. And that's what separates you from me.

"You train warriors, but I lead them. But it is not the generals who tell a people when they are ready for war. It is the leader. And you are not the leader. Thus, it is not up to you to decide whether everyone here is ready or not."

Odin paused for a brief moment. "But obviously, you want to be. Obviously, you want to lead our people into battle, to be their leader. That right to demand this is yours. But I am not willing to simply stand aside and watch you endanger them all and the fulfillment of our sacred task. You will not recklessly endanger their lives for your delusion. And as their still acting leader, it is my duty to protect them from misguided ones like you. And so I challenge you to unarmed duel."

The murmur that followed was even louder than anything before.

No one was surprised that Wolgar did not stand up directly. But if Wolgar had not stood up, he would have lost face and been banished from the community. That would have meant his death. So he had no choice but to face Odin.

Wolgar was a great fighter. He was one of the first in the community to earn the honor of wearing the Mark of the Dead. Over time, many runes had been added, showing that he was willing to go the distance and bring death to many unworthy, more than Odin. If anyone was Odin's equal, it was him.

The two men stood facing each other, as the aspirants did again and again in training, their hands bound with hemp ropes, their upper bodies free. The ring was formed by the community standing around the two opponents.

Wolgar showed from the beginning what a great fighter he was. The best of the community. He had once attacked eight unworthy people alone, weaponless, and slain them all. Everyone knew that. Odin might be the most feared of the community, but Wolgar was the one who got the most respect. The fighter everyone aspired to be, the one the aspirants had as a role model, and not just because he was their chief instructor.

"You have two minutes to get me to the ground and make sure I don't come back up," Odin said, looking at Wolgar with a look that foreboded bad things. "Two minutes in which I won't fight back. And then the two minutes end."

Odin kept his word. While Wolgar let his fists crash against him, he made no effort to fight back. Blow after blow, Wolgar landed one terrible blow after another. Odin's bearded, expressionless face kept flying around and after a short time he was bleeding from several wounds. But even when he went down, he got up again. Breathing heavily, but unwavering in his gaze, which he kept steadfastly fixed on Wolgar.

"Is that all?" sneered Odin. "Verily, this shows how inferior the inferior races are, if you were able to slay their kin so easily." Again Wolgar struck. The audience, always feasting on blood and violence, cheered, cheered him on.

Blow after blow struck Odin and he stumbled back. His eyes were already swollen, several lacerations adorned his face, but he was still standing.

"Is that all?" he shouted at Wolgar.

Wolgar's face changed color in anger and he rushed toward Odin. But his expression suddenly took on a hardness that froze the blood in the veins of anyone who saw it.

"Two!" was all he said. Then he blocked Wolgar's attack, grabbed his punching arm and simply broke it away.

While Wolgar screamed in pain, everyone else fell silent.

Odin forced Wolgar to his knees and his eyes glinted.

"By three rules we fight: No retreating! No surrender! And above all, no mercy!"

Wolgar's eyes grew wide and Odin struck. Again and again he let his right fist crash into Wolgar's face. Again and again and again. Blood splattered with each blow. The bones, already broken with the first blow, were literally bursting. With each blow, Odin turned Wolgar's *skull more into a bloody pulp, even when Wolgar was long dead and his body no longer twitched.*

It was precisely this moment, when everyone just looked at Odin in disbelief, that Finn used to escape. The guards, who had noticed what was going on, could not suppress their curiosity and were distracted. A unique chance, as no second chance would come so quickly.

Finn ran and ran. He had spent years in the impenetrable forest that he knew his way around, even in the darkness lit only by the moon. His many years of training had been designed to teach him his way around here and to find his way immediately in any unfamiliar terrain. But the same was true for his pursuers.

Of course, his absence had been noticed. He thought he could hear the dogs chasing him, but there was no typical, frightening barking. Had Odin ordered to hold them back? Probably. So Odin wanted to end it himself.

Of course, it was Gunnar, Matt and Erik who were right behind him. Finn had no doubt that they were most eager to kill him, the traitor from their own ranks who had brought so much shame upon them as well, in order to restore honor. Only because Odin had restrained them, they had not followed it before. Now, however, they were let loose, were his bloodhounds to rush Finn. Probably they had asked for it themselves, they had been waiting for it for so long.

Finn knew all too well that he could not escape them like this. They had enjoyed the same training as he, had learned lesson after lesson together with him, and were even firmer in their pursuit than he was. They would hunt him relentlessly and exploit all his weaknesses.

Finn had one goal: the north slope, which was right next to the Brunin, the raging river that led to nowhere. If he jumped in there...

Freedom was so close. Ever since he had first stood on the slope that led fifteen yards down into the raging river, he had dreamed of jumping in. To leave everything behind. And coming out as someone new.

Each of the candidates in his group had talked about the slope and had his own idea of where the river led to and what it would be like to jump into it. What it must have been like in the world outside.

Gunnar, Matt and Erik knew for sure where he was going. Therefore, they had also recognized his feint and had run directly this way. If only he had had a little more time. But that was the way it was. His way to freedom was not through Odin, but through his comrades. That's the way it was supposed to be.

It was him or them. It was that simple. No retreating. No giving up. No mercy. This was what it meant for them now, too. Odin would certainly not forgive them if they let him escape. Their lives depended on taking him down. They needed no more motivation than that. They had been taught from childhood that every fight was about their lives. More than that. The life of the community. The life of their people. To lose such a battle meant to lose everything, for themselves and for the people.

Gunnar, Matt and Erik split up. They were like well-rehearsed hunting dogs who could blindly rely on each other. Each knew his position and always knew where the others were. Finn, however, also. He had grown up with them and thus knew their ways, since he himself had once been part of their group. Which now seemed completely insane and very far away to him.

Matt was the first one he took out. It would have been easy for him to break his neck with his bare hand, which would have been the most sensible thing to do. Then he would truly have become the bringer of death to his comrade, the bane and destruction of all things seen in him. So instead he lay in wait for Matt and slammed his head with full force against a tree, so that it even seemed to tremble. But when Matt sank unconscious to the ground, he did not kill him.

Of course, the other two heard it and they knew it had gotten their comrade. Naturally, they assumed that Finn had killed him, which only increased their anger. They raised their rifles and fired, not having a clear target in mind. One bullet narrowly missed Finn.

Odin had given them rifles. Fully automatic. They must be very proud, and for that reason alone they would strive to prove themselves worthy of the honor.

Finn knew only too well what such a weapon could do. It was like a rush. He himself had not taken one with him when he fled. Everything had happened too quickly. But he had Matt's.

The obvious thing to do was to ambush the two and shoot them from cover. But he did not want that. Besides, that would steer others in his direction. Now it was just his comrades, who instinctively knew the right place, but in their eagerness to get praise from Odin, had never told anyone else about it. It was just him and them.

If he just timed it right, he could overpower them and no one would have to die today. There had already been so many deaths. He didn't want to buy his freedom with blood.

"We'll get you, traitor!" shouted Gunnar, and from his voice Finn clearly heard his hatred. He had waited too long. Too much resentment and disdain heaped upon him. Gunnar would kill him with pleasure.

With Erik it was different. Since he had not killed him in the fight, while Erik himself would have killed him without batting an eye, something was different. Erik had become quieter and had watched him again and again. He had done that before, too, as if he secretly admired him.

But since their fight, there was something else. Something that Finn couldn't grasp, but made him hope that maybe Erik wasn't approaching it with the same vigor as the others. It was only a small hope, but Finn would take anything he could get. Without hope and a little luck, there was no escaping the clutches of Odin and the Fellowship.

Gunnar fed and Erik combed the wider perimeter. They took advantage of any cover they could find, but also watched for any hiding places that might be offered to Finn. "We're going to get you, traitor!" shouted Gunnar again. "You bastard! You have disgraced us for far too long. Now it's time to settle the score!"

With that, Gunnar leapt forward and shot at the spot where he had seen the rifle barrel. Before Finn could do anything, he jumped around the tree, but there was no one there except the rifle, which was wedged in a branch fork.

"Look out!" shouted Erik still, raising his rifle.

Everything happened in a split second as Gunnar was still wondering why Erik was aiming at him. He himself pointed his gun at Erik when a branch already hit him full force in the stomach, breaking several ribs and hurling him backwards. His completely overwhelmed brain still had time to put it all together before he crashed into a tree and went down senseless. Erik had not aimed at him, but at Finn, who had hidden behind the tree, visible to Erik but not to Gunnar, and had bent a sturdy branch around so much that its force was his undoing. Erik had tried to warn him, but by then it was too late.

Finn looked at Erik, who looked at him with a frightened expression... and hesitated. In the next moment, Finn took cover, which released Erik from his stupor.

Finn closed his eyes. Erik's hesitation had saved his life, but had jeopardized Erik's for good. He had spared him, for whatever reason, but this was a fatal mistake that no one should make. He knew it. And Erik knew it, too.

"Let's stop!" shouted Finn.

Erik shook his head. "You betrayed all of us! You're a traitor! That's worse than being the member of an inferior race trying to infiltrate our people. You are a traitor to the people!"

"And you hesitated to shoot me!"

Erik swallowed. "You were too easy a target. And I didn't want to endanger my comrade."

Finn smiled mirthlessly. "We both know that's not true." He paused for a moment. "Come with me. Put it behind you. Just one jump off the cliff and we'll both be free."

Erik gripped his rifle tighter. One look was enough for Finn to see that he was wavering. But would it be enough for him to let him go? He doubted it. If only he'd had more time. But he didn't really need more time. Just a hesitation. A brief hesitation like he had just had, and he would be gone.

Erik moved closer, keeping clear of the trees and bushes that offered a perfect hiding place for an ambush. But at the same time, he also cut off Finn's path to the slope. If Finn wanted to take that path, he would have to pass him. And then everything would be settled in a single moment. Either Erik would let him go, or he would have to hurt Erik, if not kill him, in order to buy his freedom.

Finn closed his eyes. He didn't want to kill Erik. But if he had no other choice...

Carefully, he crept from tree to tree, always timing it just right. Between the edge of the forest and the edge of the slope, there was only a short free stretch. He only had to make it there, then it was only a jump into the unknown. If he got him there, they would both be able to live.

Erik was good. But he apparently still assumed that Finn wanted to kill him and had a firearm. Finn could use that to his advantage, since he could act quite differently unarmed than with a gun. All he had to do was keep the optimum distance from Erik so that his field of vision was restricted enough to take advantage of this.

Finn kept himself very low and moved even more cautiously than he would have with a real opponent, since his ultimate goal was to spare Erik's life.

Everything depended on just one moment. A moment in which everything was decided.

Erik was really good and did not make it easy for Finn. He could only hope that his former comrade was not as focused by his existing inner conflict as the situation would have required. Just a moment longer.

Suddenly Erik wheeled around, aimed right in his direction and fired. Finn just managed to dodge, but hadn't been fast enough. The bullet grazed his leg and he came down hard.

When Finn lifted his head, he could see the forest line. Behind it, the river rushed just below the slope. It was only a few more yards. It would take him only a moment to reach it. And then...

Heavy boots appeared in his field of vision, blocking his view of freedom.

Odin's boots.

In the next moment, Finn was grabbed by the collar, lifted into the air, and his face found itself in front of Odin's. Finn had seen Odin angry many times. The violence in his eyes. But never like this. His bloody face was a grimace of horror.

"You will die now!" Odin announced. "And of your death generations to come shall yet speak and feast. Let everyone see what happens to traitors!"

Odin threw Finn against a tree and pain ran through Finn's back. Already Odin was at him, ramming his fist into his stomach. Although the blow did not come unprepared, Finn could not bear its force. Odin was simply too strong, but the fight against Wolgar had cost him strength as well. Perhaps this was the only chance Finn would ever have against Odin.

Finn succeeded in blocking Odin's next blow, and in return, he placed a blow himself, directly on the laceration on his eye, which still came from Wolgar. The next blow was also successful. And the next.

Finn kicked at Odin's knee, ignoring his own pain from the graze on his leg. Odin, however, did not. As he got to his knees, his fingers reached right into the miracle.

Finn cried out in pain that exploded in white flashes in his head. Then another hard blow hit him. Instinctively, Finn blocked and struck himself. Again and again. Odin took the blows, but staggered. Only pure hatred kept him on his feet.

Odin's face was already completely covered with blood when he caught Finn's blow with his hand, twisted his arm and broke it with another blow. Finn screamed out all his despair, because he knew it was over. And then Odin kept hitting him. Breaking his ribs and bones until Finn's face was also covered in blood.

When Odin stopped hitting him, Finn no longer knew. There was only pain and the mercilessness of the world that would not allow him to pass out. He barely felt Odin grab him and slither to the edge of the slope.

"That's where you were going down?" sneered Odin with all the contempt he was capable of. "Escape from us? To freedom? What freedom? There you would have been but a slave. A slave to niggers and Kanaks who increasingly infiltrate not only this land." Odin's face was again distorted by anger. "You are a miserable traitor! I should have killed you before, but I believed you would come to your senses!"

With that, he punched Finn in the stomach again and just let him fall to the ground.

Like a giant death demon, Odin loomed over Finn, who was unable to move.

16

Anna was sweating. She entered the password again, but nothing happened. Her normal password, which she needed every day for her work, had been no problem, but the files were locked. She had no access to the data. Yesterday she had been working on it, but now suddenly everything was gone.

She turned the computer off and on again. It remained the same.

"Shit! Shit! Shit!" she screamed and was about to punch the computer, but still held back. It certainly wouldn't be a good idea to hit a computer that contained such explosive files. She might have to get someone to take care of it, in which case they would need something to work with, not a pile of junk.

When Anna heard the explosions, she knew something had gone incredibly wrong. Again.

Why had she allowed Sergey to take care of this Ben too? She should have insisted that he just shoot him. But she had seen it in Sergey's eyes that he had not been satisfied with that. And she knew all too well that if you wanted to prevent men like Sergey from satisfying their needs on you, you had better give them what they wanted.

And now she heard explosions. This could not be a coincidence.

She would have liked too much to believe that it was a coincidence. That none of this meant anything. Or that Russev's people were simply covering their tracks. Something like that. But she knew better.

Ben had done it. She didn't know how, but he was still alive. And if he was alive, he was looking for her. For sure. And he knew where to find her, too.

Actually, she would have been long gone. But Mo had to have done something. Of course, he knew something like that. He was a damn genius at computers and had always made sure that the IT department in her branch had the least to do, which had always been just fine with her. But now he had used his knowledge to lock all the important files.

Anna had tried desperately to open them. And the longer it took, the more nervous she became.

She had to open them. Everything depended on it. If she couldn't get the data to the accounts, then...

She felt a chill run down her spine.

No, she couldn't think about that.

She had always imagined everything so well. Problems included. But what had happened that night, she hadn't seen that before. How could she?

Actually, everything could have ended with Mo. A regrettable loss, which she would have liked to prevent, but equally accepted. The whole thing would still have been uncomfortable, but not like this. Of course, she would have had to finally get rid of Russev and Ahrend. But everything according to her schedule and not so bang on the spot.

It had all been planned. Her whole exit strategy. And also how it was to continue.

And it could all still happen. She just needed access to the data. Just that and she would sort it all out. But access remained denied to her.

Again and again, she glanced at the clock. Listened to the sirens wailing in the distance. Her time was running out. And everything she had built up would be irretrievably destroyed.

When she looked to the side in the main branch room, Ben was standing there.

She jumped up in shock, causing her desk chair to bang against a shelf. In the next moment, she searched for her pistol in near panic. When she found it, she held it out, aiming at Ben, but he made no move.

They stood there for a few moments. Anna with the gun at hand. And Ben, whom she was threatening, who looked as if he had just escaped from hell. His eyes fixed on her made her gulp. His look was unambiguous.

"Who the hell are you?!" she finally screamed out her anger. "Who are you?!"

Ben didn't move. "Nobody!"

Anna screamed. "Cut the crap! You're not a banker!"

"Yes, I am."

Anna almost pulled the trigger because of the answer. "Stop it! Tell me who the fuck you are!"

Ben remained unmoved. "I'm the one whose friend you killed."

Anna's face contorted in anger. "I already told you! It wasn't planned! He didn't fucking let up and put me and everyone in danger!"

"He trusted you. He even sent me to protect you." Ben paused, then gave a short cynical laugh.

"What?!" Anna wanted to know.

"Maybe he figured out your secret, too. Realized when he saw everything in front of him that something was wrong. And sent me to you because he knew what would happen."

Anna's jaws ground. "You mean he sent you to me knowing that this is exactly what was going to happen?" Again she paused. "Why? How did he know that? How did he know that you would destroy everything and leave only corpses in your wake? And that you would get behind this? Behind me and what I've done? How?"

Ben smiled. "Because he was Mo. There was no one who knew me that well. Except for his father. Mo always saw me right. Better than I saw myself."

Anna took a breath. "Well, what the fuck does that mean? What did he see? Who are you?"

Ben smiled wearily. "If I told you, you wouldn't believe it. It doesn't matter, either. What only matters is that you killed Mo, and I'm going to kill you for it."

"Um, now this is the part where I have to step in," a voice suddenly sounded.

Confused, Anna saw a man she didn't know enter. Wolters kept his hands raised in plain sight next to his body and came closer to stand near Ben.

"Who are you?" Anna wanted to know, aiming the pistol at him. The man had to be around fifty, wore a gray suit and looked more like a diplomat with his well-groomed appearance. But there was something impenetrable in his eyes. Something dangerous that made Anna instinctively swallow.

Wolters acted innocent. "Who, me? Who am I? Hmm. Nobody. I'm not here at all. And you'd better forget you ever saw me." He paused for a moment, as if considering. "Well, actually, you'd better have forgotten about bringing up criminal business. If you had, people wouldn't have died and we wouldn't be sitting here in this situation."

Anna seemed more and more overwhelmed. "Are you a fucking cop?! Also an undercover guy like him?!"

Wolters was surprised and looked at Ben uncomprehendingly, then turned back to Anna and pointed at Ben. "He an undercover cop? Did you see all the damage he did? The whole factory's on fire and he's turned this peaceful little town here into a Chicago back in the thirties. He's truly anything but a cop!"

Anna gripped her gun tighter and Wolters reflexively raised his hands a little higher.

"What are you doing here?" Wolters smiled. "That's a much better question. Very good." With that, he turned to Ben. "I came to tell you that I can't allow you to kill her. I'm sorry, I can't allow that."

Ben remained motionless as Anna nervously stepped from one foot to the other.

"He, kill me? I'm the one with the gun! You should rather say that I shouldn't kill him. Which is all the same now."

Wolters screwed up his face and shook his head. "No, I'm sorry. My message was already meant for him. But perhaps I should point out that I certainly won't intervene and restrain him if you try to kill him. There is a case to be made against murder. Nothing at all against self-defense resulting in death."

"Murder?" asked Ben.

Wolters rolled his eyes. "We both know she doesn't stand a chance. Thus, it would be murder."

"She had Mo killed!"

Wolters' face turned sad. "Yes. I know. That explains all the sweating you've been doing, and my being here. But I can't let you kill her."

Ben nodded. "I don't have to."

With that, he slowly pulled out a sheet similar to the one Anna already knew.

"What's this?" she asked, irritated.

Ben smiled weakly. "The mail addresses from the Grimms. I contacted them with Sergey's cell phone. When he did, I informed them that you had robbed them of their money. I guess they've already contacted you about that, which is why you're so nervous."

Anna gulped and rose again from one moment to the next, confirming Ben's suspicions.

Wolters laughed out loud. "Oh, lady, you're in big trouble!"

Ben nodded. "I explained to them that it was you who screwed them all by hiring a hit man to take them all out. I guess once it becomes public that Russev, Matteo, and Sergey are dead, they won't doubt the authenticity of the message."

Anna turned chalk white. "You can't do that!"

"I already have." He was silent for a moment. "You won't be able to feel safe anywhere. There's a gruesome death lurking around every corner. They're all specialists in the art of killing. They know how to kill a person slowly and extra painfully or keep them alive forever. I guess the brutal guys who took your father were among your clients, too?"

Wolters seemed to be thinking as Anna grew more agitated.

"So we don't have access to the damning data on this computer?"

Ben nodded. "Mo locked everything down with a special code. He died with it."

Anna's eyes grew wide. "That's not true! He knows the code! Both used it all the time! Ask him! Look at him! You must know him!"

Ben didn't move and Wolters maintained his feigned seriousness.

"I guess you, Ms. Kerkov, have covered your tracks well too, so they can't connect you to the whole events, since no one is alive to witness it."

"What?! Ben can! He was there everywhere!"

Wolters shook his head. "I never got used to that name." Then he looked at Anna. "Unfortunately, this man is under my supervision and has never been here because of it. I advise you to forget you ever saw him. In return, I am committed to having you connected with everything. Assuming a full statement from you. Thus you are guaranteed a long spell in prison. And thus your angry business partners will not be able to get at you."

Now Anna looked at Wolters. She wanted to say something, but she couldn't. She was trembling from head to toe, and although there was a danger that she might fire the pistol quite unintentionally, both men turned and left the room. Behind them they heard Anna scream.

As Ben stepped out of the store, he saw men from special police units in full body armor everywhere, pointing their guns in their direction, but neither he nor Wolters paid any attention to them and just kept walking.

"I thought you were going to keep quiet," Wolters said, looking up at the sky lit by the fire in the factory.

"They killed Mo."

Wolters nodded. "I understand. But I'm afraid there are consequences."

Ben nodded. "Everything in life has consequences. Some things are worth their consequences."

With that, he turned to Wolters. "Mo was the straw that always kept me rooted in the here and now. I can't escape my past. It will never be possible. But Mo always grounded me. Put everything into perspective. He kept in me the belief that another life is possible and that I could find peace. Not today. Not tomorrow. But someday, for sure."

Wolters pressed his lips together. "I'm sorry. I'll do my best to keep you out of here."

Ben nodded. "And if not, let them come. And they will."

Wolters shook his head and Ben walked away. He paid no attention to the people. A police officer tried to stop him, but Wolters just raised his hand and the officer let him through.

The head of operations of the local police came up to Wolters and looked at him angrily. "What are you doing? First you just march in there like that. Then you decide who gets to go and who doesn't. Who do you think you are?"

Wolters smiled and turned around only briefly, whereupon a policeman came up to him, whom the head of operations recognized directly as a high-ranking member of the State Security.

"What is the State Security doing here? And who the hell are you?" the officer-in-charge asked, irritated.

The man from the State Security answered instead of Wolters.

"This man was never here."

The operations manager blushed. "And what about the other man? The one who looks like..."

"What man?"

"Well, the one who was just allowed to leave. The one my officer was supposed to let through?"

Wolters turned to the policeman in question. "Did you just let a man through?"

The officer shook his head. "No. No one came through here."

The officer-in-charge turned a deep red. "What the hell is going on here?"

Wolters smiled and got up close to the operations officer. "That's not the question. The question is what can I do? And what can you do?

"Here's what I can do, for example: I make a call and you stand by the road starting tomorrow and secure the route to school.

"This depends on what you can do. And that is this: can you forget that you saw me and some ominous man and the state protection here? Or can you not?"

Wolters saw how the jaw of the head of operations grimaced and his eyes flashed. But he seemed to be thinking very carefully about his next words.

"What man?" he finally said.

Wolters smiled and patted him on the shoulder. "Very good. I would suggest you send a female officer in there. There she will meet a young woman, very eager to make an arrest, who has quite a bit to say and who will explain the whole mess. The best thing to do is to get in touch with the Organized Crime Division immediately. I don't know, I'm not that familiar with it. I'm just a layman. I don't even know what's going on."

A shot rang out from the store and everyone turned to look. The officers took cover and aimed at the entrance and windows, but they were all intact and no one appeared.

"Hmm, it could also be that you better send in some paramedics. Ms. Kerkov might have done something stupid. Or, from her point of view, something very consistent."

With that, he nodded to the dispatcher, turned and left.

The policeman who had not stopped Ben now let him through as well, and Wolters tapped his forehead in thanks.

Ben was already barely visible. He kept walking, oblivious to his injuries and to the people standing in the street, not quite knowing which way to look, since on one side the factory was burning and on the other something big had happened at the local bank branch.

Slowly Ben realized that everything was hurting him. He needed to get his injuries treated, but right now he just wanted to get away.

When was the last time he had felt like this?

When he first met Wolters?

Probably.

Everything had changed that day.

It had also been Wolters who had addressed him with his real name for the last time. Since then, he had given himself another one and tried to fill it with life and live up to it. Ben. The name of a true friend. But like Mo, this name had probably died the previous night.

"What has happened here sounds unbelievable," explained the experienced field reporter, who was standing near the small bank branch while police officers ran back and forth around her. "According to various sources, the numerous dead are members of the Russian mafia, including clan boss Russev, whose goings-on came to an end here. According to various eyewitnesses, a single man is believed to be responsible, who at the moment is likely to be questioned by police about the incidents."

A picture of Ben faded in, a snapshot, not a good one, but probably enhanced by various filtering programs.

"This is the man who, in all likelihood, single-handedly confronted and took out the Russian mafia. Neither he nor the police are available for comment at this time."

17

Daron looked at the screen of his cell phone. If he had any doubts before, they were completely dispelled when he looked at the message. Their contact had sent them a recording that gave a much clearer picture of the man, and Daron breathed a sigh of relief. As soon as he saw the recording, he knew who it was. And he knew the old man wanted to see it.

Daron stroked his full beard. Then he took the tablet with the frozen image and walked over to the hut. When he knocked, no one asked him to come in, but no one told him to stay out either.

As soon as he entered the shack, he stopped in surprise, because the six screens on the walls showed the various news stations, all reporting on the one event. On each screen, the particular report was frozen, each showing the photo of Ben in different qualitative resolutions.

Daron looked at the screens and then looked to the large, leather office chair where the old man sat as if on a throne, gazing fixedly at the TVs. When the man with the bald skull looked to the side, Daron saw again the milky-blind eye and the thin scar running across it.

Daron stepped forward and handed Odin the tablet.

"This is from our police liaison," he explained briefly, and Odin took the tablet in his paw-like hands to look at it closely. A smile played around the corner of his mouth.

"Welcome back, Erik."

<h1 style="text-align:center">18</h1>

"Erik!" Odin called out.

Erik, who had watched everything that had happened between Odin and Finn with an increasingly pale face, joined his leader on the slope.

Odin grabbed Finn again and lifted him up to hold him out to Erik. "Draw your knife!" Odin ordered.

Erik looked at him, then pulled out his knife. It had a large blade and had been hardened with his own blood, which had made him very proud. It was the first weapon he had been given. Now, however, it only filled him with terror.

"Put an end to the traitor as he deserves!" Odin continued. "Stab him like a mangy mutt and rip out his guts!"

Erik's eyes grew wide with horror. He wanted to say something, but how could he? This was Odin. Their leader. Their protector. The one who had just slain a man with his bare hands and had done the same to Finn.

Finn, however, was still alive, even if this hardly seemed possible. And in his eyes, which looked at Erik, he saw the most terrible thing he had ever seen, which went through him and gave him a mad stab in the heart: forgiveness.

Erik shook his head imperceptibly. He looked at Finn, whose expression was full of kindness, and then at Odin, a face of hatred.

Before Erik realized what was happening, Odin threw Finn at Erik. Finn's limp body slammed into Erik and he felt his knife slide unresistingly into Finn's body, deep to the hilt.

Erik had never experienced such terror. He didn't even know how to move. Just wanted to get Finn to the ground as gently as he could, as if that would change anything. But it didn't.

As he laid Finn on the sparse grass, Erik clearly saw the last shred of life drain from him. His face showed only pain, but his eyes, which remained fixed on Erik, were still full of kindness and understanding. And while everything was falling apart for Erik, Finn was dying.

Erik stared at Finn's body. He had killed the one who had spared him. And why had he looked at him like that? Erik couldn't understand. Why hadn't Finn just killed him? Then he would have escaped. Been free. Wha...

"Loser!"

The one word delivered with a contempt that knew no bounds brought Erik back from his torpor. Looking up, he saw the hateful grimace of Odin, who only looked more like a demon because of all the blood.

Without thinking, Erik grabbed the handle of the knife that was still stuck in Finn's body, pulled it out, and ran the blade around. He felt a brief resistance as the razor-sharp blade cut through Odin's thigh.

Screaming, Odin went to his knees. Then his face became contorted with rage again and he wanted to reach for Erik. Erik, however, had expected this and let the blade move again, so that it cut into Odin's arm. Odin cried out again and when he turned his face back to Erik, the blade cut across his face and split his left eye.

Screaming as if out of his mind, Odin fell to the side.

Erik looked at him, then stood up, grabbed Finn's body without thinking and jumped with him into the icy waters.